Whispers of Fate

By Chantelle Dykhoff

There are whispers in the air—
soft as moonlight, wild as wolves.
They call to the dreamers,
the broken-hearted,
the ones who believe
that love is never just a coincidence—
it's fate.

Follow your heart.
Even when the path is dark.
Even when it howls.

Writing this story has been my escape—
from heartache,
from hard days,
into a world where magic still lingers
and soulmates find each other
against all odds.

Thank you for holding this book in your hands.
For stepping into this world with me.
For believing in love,
in legends,
and in second chances.

Now—
come closer.
The forest is waiting.

Prologue: The Awakening

The moon hung heavy over the quiet town of Kaiapoi, casting a silvery glow across the still waters of the Waimakariri River. In the distance, the Southern Alps loomed, their snowcapped peaks illuminated by the faint light. The night felt alive—an electric hum buzzing through the air, though few could sense it.

Inside a small, weathered house on the edge of town, Lara Matheson lay in bed, staring at the ceiling. Sleep refused to come, her body restless and burning with an energy she couldn't explain. Her wolf stirred, silent yet present, just as it had been for as long as she could remember.

But tonight was different.

Lara's hands trembled as a strange warmth pulsed from the necklace around her neck. It had been a gift from her nana before she passed, a delicate silver chain with a pendant shaped like a crescent moon. For years, it had been nothing more than a comforting keepsake, a piece of her nana to hold onto. Now, it glowed faintly in the dark, its light pulsing in time with her racing heartbeat.

A sharp pain tore through her chest, and she gasped, clutching her sides.

Her wolf's voice echoed in her mind for the first time. *"We are one now."*

Chapter 1: A New Beginning

The morning light filtered through the lace curtains of Lara's bedroom, pulling her from restless dreams. She sat up slowly, her body sore as if she'd run a marathon.

Her wolf stirred beneath the surface, a new presence that felt foreign yet familiar. Every sound in the house seemed amplified—the clatter of plates in the kitchen, the hum of her dad's radio in the garage. The air carried a thousand scents she had never noticed before: the faint saltiness of the river breeze, the damp earth outside her window, and the lavender detergent her mum used on the laundry.

"Lara, breakfast!" her mum called from the kitchen.

"Coming!" Lara replied, her voice shaky.

She stumbled to the bathroom and stared at her reflection. Her dark brown hair hung in loose waves around her face, and her usually hazel eyes seemed to glow faintly gold in the morning light. She leaned closer, heart pounding. Was she imagining things?
"Pull yourself together," she muttered, splashing cold water on her face.

A Birthday Breakfast

Lara shuffled into the kitchen, greeted by the smell of bacon and pancakes. Her dad, a tall man with a gruff demeanour, sat at the table, sipping his coffee. Her mum hovered by the stove, humming a tune as she flipped the pancakes.

“Happy birthday, sweetheart,” her dad said with a rare smile, sliding a neatly wrapped box across the table.

Lara forced a smile, trying to ignore the strange sensations coursing through her. “Thanks, Dad.”

Her mum set a plate of pancakes in front of her, leaning down to kiss her cheek. “Eighteen! Can you believe it? It feels like just yesterday you were climbing trees in the backyard.”

Lara chuckled, though her wolf growled softly in the back of her mind, impatient and restless.
She unwrapped the gift—a leather-bound journal with her initials embossed on the cover. Her dad cleared his throat. “Thought you might like something to keep track of your… thoughts.”

“Thanks,” Lara said, running her fingers over the smooth cover.

Her mum sat down, her face softening. “How are you feeling today? Any… changes?”

Lara hesitated, glancing down at her glowing necklace. “I’m fine,” she lied. “Just a bit tired.”

Her parents exchanged a look, but neither pressed further.

School Arrival

Kaiapoi High School wasn’t large—only a few hundred students—and by now, Lara knew nearly everyone. As she parked her battered Toyota in the school lot, she spotted her best friends, Kate and Lilly, waiting near the entrance.

Kate was tall and athletic; her blonde hair pulled back into a messy bun. She waved enthusiastically as Lara approached. "Happy birthday, wolf-girl!"

Lilly, shorter and more reserved, smiled warmly. "How does it feel to be an adult?"

"Like every other day," Lara said with a grin, though her wolf bristled at the half-truth. The girls fell into step together, chatting about their weekend plans as they headed to their lockers. Lara's wolf remained restless, scanning the crowd as if searching for something—or someone.

Then she saw him.

He was leaning against the far wall, arms crossed over his chest, his dark hair falling into his eyes. He was tall, with sharp features and an air of confidence that set him apart. Jessie, he's back.

"Who's that?" Kate asked, nudging Lara.

"Jessie," Lara replied, though her wolf stirred at the sight of him, a low growl vibrating in her chest. She hadn't seen him in a long time.
As if sensing her gaze, Jessie turned, his piercing blue eyes locking onto hers. For a moment, the world seemed to still. Lara's wolf growled louder, a mix of warning and intrigue.

Jessie smirked, his eyes flicking to her necklace before returning to her face. He gave a small nod, as if acknowledging something only the two of them could understand and walked away.

"Okay, what was that?" Lilly asked, wide-eyed.

"I have no idea," Lara said, her heart racing.

The Mysterious Newcomer

Throughout the day, Jessie seemed to pop up wherever Lara went. At first, she thought it was a coincidence. He sat three rows behind her in English class; his sharp eyes fixed on her whenever she dared to glance back. In the hallway between periods, he brushed past her, his shoulder lightly grazing hers, leaving a spark of something she couldn't explain. Jessie was older now and has filled out.

By lunch, the air between them felt charged, and her wolf was pacing restlessly in her mind.

"Seriously, who is this guy?" Kate whispered, leaning across the cafeteria table.

Lilly shrugged. "I heard he just transferred from Auckland. His dad's in forestry or something."
"Whatever it is, he's definitely not just some random guy," Kate said, raising an eyebrow at Lara. "He hasn't stopped looking at you all day."

Lara rolled her eyes, trying to appear unfazed. "It's probably nothing. Maybe he's just… curious, we knew each other a while ago."

Kate snorted. "Right. Curious about *you*. Don't act like you didn't notice the way he was staring at your necklace in English class."

ara's hand instinctively went to the pendant resting against her chest. The glow had faded since the morning, but she couldn't shake the feeling that Jessie had noticed it—and that it meant something to him.

An Unexpected Meeting

After school, Lara decided to walk to the edge of town, needing to clear her head. The woods called to her, as they always did when she felt overwhelmed.

The path was quiet, the late afternoon sun filtering through the trees. Birds chirped overhead, and the distant sound of the river provided a soothing backdrop.

Her wolf urged her to shift, to let go of her human form and run free, but Lara resisted. She wasn't ready—not yet.

She was so lost in her thoughts that she didn't notice the figure leaning against a tree ahead until she was nearly on top of him.
"Skipping track practice already?" Jessie's voice was smooth, his tone teasing.

Lara stopped short, her heart pounding. "What are you doing here?"
He shrugged, pushing off the tree and closing the distance between them. "I could ask you the same thing."

"I come here all the time," she said, crossing her arms defensively. "You don't."

Jessie smirked. “Maybe I just wanted to see what all the fuss was about. After all, it’s been many years since we last spoke and I can’t help myself seeing your mysterious necklace… seemed worth investigating.”

Her wolf growled at the edge of his words, sensing a challenge. Lara clenched her fists, fighting to stay calm. “I don’t know what you think you know about me, but—”

“I know enough,” Jessie interrupted, his voice softening. “Like the fact that you’re not just an ordinary girl. You can feel it, can’t you? That pull between us?” “She feels it in her bones and in the low growl of her wolf—a quiet, magnetic pull toward him, not born of longing but of recognition, as if their paths were carved by the same unseen hand.”

“I don’t know what you’re talking about,” she said, turning to leave.

“Lara,” Jessie called after her, his voice firm. “You’re not the only one with secrets.”

She froze, her heart pounding. Slowly, she turned back to face him.

“What do you mean?”
Jessie stepped closer, his blue eyes piercing hers. “I’m just saying… maybe we have more in common than you think.”

Before she could respond, he turned and walked away, leaving her standing alone in the woods.

Dreams of the Wolf

That night, Lara dreamed of the forest. She was running, her wolf's paws pounding against the earth as she weaved through the trees. The moonlight guided her, illuminating the path ahead.

But she wasn't alone.
A shadowy figure ran beside her, its movements strong and fluid. She couldn't see its face, but she could feel its presence—a mix of power and familiarity that made her heart race.

Her necklace glowed brightly, its light cutting through the darkness.

"Lara." The voice was low and urgent, calling her name.

She woke with a start, her heart hammering in her chest. The room was dark, but the faint glow of her necklace lit up the space around her.

"What is happening to me?" she whispered, clutching the pendant tightly.

A Tense Reunion

The next morning, Lara was determined to avoid Jessie at all costs. But by third period, it was clear he wasn't going to make that easy.

"Morning, Lara," he said, sliding into the seat next to hers in History class.
She glared at him. "What do you want?"

Jessie smirked, leaning back in his chair. "You looked like you could use some company."

"Not from you."

His grin widened, but his eyes held a hint of seriousness. "Look, I get it. You're freaked out. But trust me when I say you're not the only one going through… changes."
Her wolf stirred at his words, and Lara's frustration bubbled over. "I don't know what game you're playing, but I don't have time for it."

Jessie leaned in, his voice dropping to a whisper. "This isn't a game, Lara. And whether you like it or not, you are part of something bigger now."

Before she could respond, the teacher called for silence, and Jessie leaned back, satisfied.

A Threat Revealed

After school, Lara met up with Kate and Lilly at their usual spot by the river. The sun was setting, casting golden light across the water.
"You are quiet today," Kate said, nudging Lara with her elbow. "Still thinking about the new guy?"

Lilly frowned. "He's… intense. Do you think he knows about… you know?"

Lara hesitated, her fingers brushing her necklace. "I don't know what he knows. But he's hiding something, that's for sure."

As they talked, the shadows around them seemed to grow longer, darker. Lara's wolf perked up, sensing danger.

"Do you hear that?" she asked, her voice low.

Kate and Lilly froze, straining to listen.

A low growl echoed through the trees.

"Lara…" Lilly whispered, her eyes wide with fear.

Before they could react, a pair of glowing yellow eyes appeared in the darkness.
Lara's necklace flared to life, its light cutting through the shadows like a beacon. The creature snarled, retreating slightly, but it didn't leave.

"We need to go," Lara said, her voice steady despite the fear coursing through her.

The three girls ran, the sound of paws crashing through the underbrush close behind them.
Just as they reached the edge of the woods, a figure stepped into their path.

"Jessie?" Lara gasped, skidding to a stop.

He didn't answer. His eyes glowed faintly, and his stance was protective as he stepped between the girls and the creature.

"Stay behind me," he said, his voice low and commanding.

Before Lara could process what was happening, Jessie lunged at the creature, moving with inhuman speed.

The Confrontation

Jessie's movement was a blur, faster than anything Lara had ever seen. One moment he was standing protectively in front of them, and the next, he was grappling with the shadowy creature.

The beast snarled—a guttural, feral sound that sent chills down Lara's spine. It was massive, easily the size of a small bear, with thick black fur and glowing yellow eyes that burned with malevolence. Its claws raked through the air, aiming for Jessie's chest, but he dodged with a speed that defied logic.

Lara's instincts screamed at her to intervene. Her wolf roared in her mind, urging her to shift and fight, but fear held her frozen. She could only watch as Jessie landed a powerful punch to the creature's side, sending it stumbling back.

"Run!" Jessie shouted over his shoulder, his voice harsh and commanding. "Get out of here!"
Kate grabbed Lara's arm, pulling her toward the path. "Come on, Lara! We need to go!"

“No,” Lara said, shaking her head. Her necklace glowed brighter, its light pulsing in rhythm with her racing heart. Something inside her told her she couldn’t leave.

The creature lunged at Jessie again, its jaws snapping dangerously close to his face. This time, Jessie wasn’t quick enough to dodge entirely. The beast’s claws raked across his arm, drawing blood. He winced but didn’t falter, his movements precise and controlled as he drove the creature back with a series of rapid strikes.

“Lara, we have to help him!” Lilly cried, her voice trembling.
Kate looked pale; her usual confidence shaken. “And do what? He’s faster than anything I’ve ever seen. We’ll just get in the way.”

Lara clenched her fists, her wolf pushing harder against the barrier in her mind. She could feel its power coursing through her veins, begging to be unleashed.

Let me out, the wolf growled. *He needs us.*
Her gaze snapped back to Jessie, who was still holding his own against the creature but beginning to tire. The beast seemed to sense his weakness, pressing its advantage with relentless attacks.

Lara took a deep breath and stepped forward.

“Lara, no!” Kate shouted, grabbing at her arm, but Lara shook her off.

Her wolf surged forward, and this time, she didn’t fight it.

The Shift

The transformation was both exhilarating and terrifying. Heat flooded her body as her bones shifted and reshaped. Her vision sharpened, the colours of the world dimming but every detail becoming crystal clear. Her hearing and sense of smell heightened, and the familiar hum of the forest became an overwhelming symphony

Within seconds, Lara stood on four legs instead of two. Her sleek, golden-brown fur gleamed in the light of her glowing necklace, and her wolf instincts took over.

The creature paused mid-attack, its yellow eyes locking onto Lara. It growled, its hackles rising in challenge.

Jessie froze, his blue eyes widening in shock. "Lara?"

Lara ignored him, focusing on the creature in front of her. Her wolf growled low in her throat, stepping forward with calculated precision.

The beast lunged, but Lara was faster. She darted to the side, her claws digging into the earth as she twisted to strike. Her teeth sank into the creature's shoulder, and it howled in pain, flailing wildly to throw her off.
Jessie took advantage of the distraction, launching himself at the beast's exposed side. Together, they drove it back, their combined attacks forcing it to retreat.
The fight was brutal and chaotic, but Lara felt a strange sense of clarity. Her wolf instincts guided her every move, anticipating the creature's attacks and countering with deadly precision.

Finally, with a vicious bite to its neck, Lara forced the creature to the ground. Jessie moved in for the finishing blow, a silver dagger flashing in his hand.

The beast snarled one last time before going still, its body crumbling into ash beneath their combined efforts.

The Aftermath

Lara shifted back into her human form, collapsing to her knees as the adrenaline left her body. She was trembling, her hands covered in dirt and sweat, but she was alive.

Jessie crouched beside her, his expression a mix of concern and disbelief.

"What the hell was that?" he asked, his voice rough.

"I could ask you the same thing," Lara shot back, her breath coming in ragged gasps.

Jessie's gaze dropped to her glowing necklace. "That's no ordinary trinket you've got there."

Lara clutched the pendant tightly, her mind racing. "You knew about this, didn't you? About me?"

Jessie hesitated, running a hand through his messy hair. "I suspected. But I didn't think you'd shift like that—at least not yet."

"What do you mean, 'not yet'?" Lara demanded.

Before Jessie could answer, Kate and Lilly burst through the trees, their faces pale with fear.

"Are you okay?" Lilly asked, dropping to her knees beside Lara.

"We saw… everything," Kate said, her voice shaking. "Lara, you're… a wolf."

Lara looked between her friends and Jessie, her mind spinning. "I'll explain everything," she said finally. "But first, I need answers."

Jessie nodded; his jaw tight. "Then we'd better talk. But not here. It's not safe."

Unravelling the Mystery

Back at Lara's house, the group gathered in her small living room. Her parents were out for the evening, leaving them alone to piece together what had happened.

Jessie paced the room, his injured arm hastily bandaged. "That wasn't just a random rogue," he said, his tone serious. "That thing was sent here—probably for you."
"Sent by who?" Lara asked, still clutching her necklace.
Jessie stopped pacing, his gaze locking on hers. "There's someone out there—someone dangerous. And they're after whatever power that necklace holds."

Lara's stomach twisted. "What does this have to do with me?"

Jessie's expression softened slightly. "Because you're not just a wolf, Lara. You're something more. And whoever sent that creature knows it."

The Mystery Deepens

Jessie's words hung in the air, heavy with unspoken truths. Lara's heart pounded as she stared at him, trying to make sense of what he was saying.

"Something more?" she echoed, her voice barely above a whisper. Jessie nodded; his piercing blue eyes unwavering. "You're not like the others, Lara. Not even like me. That necklace isn't just some family heirloom—it's a key. A beacon. And tonight, it just announced to the world that you're awake."
"Awake?" Lara frowned, her wolf stirring uneasily. "I don't understand. You're talking in riddles. What am I?"

Jessie sighed, running a hand through his hair. "I was hoping we'd have more time before this all started. But now that they know you've shifted…"

"Who's 'they'?" Kate interrupted; her voice sharp with fear. She stood near the doorway with her arms crossed, her usual confidence overshadowed by the lingering shock of what she'd seen.

Jessie hesitated, glancing at Kate, then back at Lara. "Rogues, like the one tonight. Creatures who've given up any shred of humanity for power. But there's something worse out there—someone who's been waiting for you."

The room fell silent, Jessie's words sinking in like cold water.

Lilly, who had been quiet until now, spoke up hesitantly. "But why Lara? What makes her so special?"
Jessie exhaled sharply, clearly reluctant to answer. He paced again; his footsteps heavy on the worn carpet. Finally, he stopped and looked directly at Lara.

"Because your wolf isn't just any wolf," he said. "It's tied to something ancient—something powerful. And that necklace? It's the last piece of the puzzle."

Lara's hand instinctively went to her pendant, her fingers curling around the crescent moon. It felt warm against her skin, pulsing faintly, as if in response to Jessie's words.

"This doesn't make sense," Lara said, shaking her head. "I've had this necklace my whole life. It's just… a gift from my nana."

"No," Jessie said firmly. "It's not. It's a seal—a barrier holding back something your nana fought to protect. And now that you've shifted, the seal is starting to weaken."

The room grew colder, the shadows seeming to stretch longer as the weight of Jessie's words settled over them.

"What happens when it breaks?" Lara asked, her voice steady despite the fear rising in her chest.

Jessie's jaw tightened. "If it breaks, it won't just be you in danger. It'll be all of us."

The Wolf's Warning

Before Lara could press him further, a sharp growl echoed in her mind, making her flinch. Her wolf's voice, low and urgent, growled words she didn't fully understand.

"He knows. But not all. Be ready. The shadows come."

"Lara?" Lilly asked, concern in her voice. "Are you okay?"

Lara blinked, realizing she'd been gripping the armrest of the couch so tightly her knuckles were white. "Yeah," she said quickly. "I'm fine."

But she wasn't. Her wolf was restless, pacing in the back of her mind like a caged animal. And for the first time, Lara wondered if it wasn't just restless—if it was afraid.

Jessie seemed to notice her unease. He crouched in front of her, his voice softening. "Lara, I know this is a lot. But you need to trust me. If we're going to survive this, we have to work together."

She looked at him, searching his face for answers. Despite the tension between them, there was something in his eyes that made her want to believe him.

Before she could respond, the faint sound of a door creaking open interrupted the moment.

Everyone froze.

"What was that?" Kate whispered, her voice barely audible.

Jessie's head snapped toward the hallway, his entire body tensing.
"Stay here," he said, his voice low and commanding.
"Jessie—" Lara began, but he cut her off with a sharp look.

"I mean it, Lara. Don't move."

He rose to his feet, moving silently toward the hallway. The air felt thick with tension, the shadows in the room seeming to press closer.

An Unseen Threat

Lara's necklace flared to life, its glow cutting through the darkness. Her wolf growled low in her mind; the warning clear.

"Danger. Close."

Jessie stopped in his tracks, his eyes narrowing as he stared into the shadows. "Who's there?" he demanded, his voice steady but laced with authority.
For a moment, there was nothing but silence. Then, a faint whisper drifted through the air, sending chills down Lara's spine.

"The girl... the key..."

Jessie moved faster than Lara thought possible, lunging toward the source of the sound. But when he reached the doorway, there was nothing there—only empty air.

"What the hell was that?" Kate whispered, her face pale.

Jessie returned to the room; his expression grim. “They’re here. Watching.”

“Who’s watching?” Lara asked, rising to her feet.

Jessie’s gaze locked on hers, and for the first time, she saw genuine fear in his eyes.

“They know where you are now,” he said. “And they won’t stop until they have you.”

Chapter 2: Shadows and Secrets

The morning sun broke over Kaiapoi, spilling golden light across the sleepy town. Lara stood in the woods behind her house, the crisp air biting at her skin as she waited for Jessie to arrive.

Her body still ached from their sparring session the day before, but she wasn't about to let that stop her. If Jessie was right—if more dangers were coming—she needed to be ready.

The sound of footsteps crunching on the underbrush pulled her from her thoughts. Jessie stepped into the clearing, his usual confident smirk in place.

"Ready for round two?" he asked, tossing her a bottle of water.

Lara caught it, glaring at him. "You didn't exactly go easy on me yesterday."

"Why would I?" Jessie replied, crossing his arms. "The rogues won't go easy on you, either. And like I said, you're strong. But strength means nothing if you don't know how to use it."

Lara rolled her eyes. "Fine. Let's get this over with."

Training with Jessie

Jessie didn't hold back.

For hours, he pushed Lara to her limits, teaching her how to anticipate attacks, how to use her wolf's instincts to her advantage, and how to control her strength without letting it control her.

"Focus," Jessie said as they circled each other, his stance relaxed but ready. "You're thinking too much. Trust your instincts."

Lara lunged at him, her movements fluid but predictable. Jessie sidestepped easily, grabbing her arm and twisting her around until her back hit the ground.
"Too slow," he said, standing over her.

Lara growled, her wolf bristling with frustration. "You're impossible."

Jessie grinned, offering her a hand. "And you're stubborn. But that's not a bad thing."

Lara took his hand reluctantly, her cheeks flushing as he pulled her to her feet. His touch lingered just a moment longer than necessary, and for a brief second, their eyes met.

Her heart skipped a beat, but Jessie quickly released her hand, stepping back.

"Take five," he said, his tone casual, though there was a hint of something in his expression—something he wasn't saying.

A New Mystery

After training, Lara walked to school with Kate and Lilly, her body sore but her mind sharper than ever.

“You’re glowing,” Kate teased, bumping Lara’s shoulder. “What’s got you all smiley today?”

“I’m not smiling,” Lara said quickly, though she felt warmth creeping into her cheeks.

“You totally are,” Kate said, laughing. “It’s Jessie, isn’t it? You’ve been spending a lot of time with him lately.”

Lara shot her a look. “It’s not like that. He’s helping me with… stuff.”

“Uh-huh,” Kate said, smirking. “Sure, he is.”

Lilly changed the subject, sensing Lara’s discomfort. “Have you noticed anything… strange around school lately?”

“Strange how?” Lara asked.

Lilly hesitated, glancing around nervously. “I don’t know. It’s probably nothing. Just… sometimes I feel like someone’s watching.”

Lara frowned, her wolf stirring uneasily. “You’ve felt that, too?”

Kate waved a hand dismissively. “You’re both being paranoid. This is Kaiapoi, not some big city. Who’s going to be creeping around here?”
But as they reached the school gates, Lara’s wolf tensed, her senses sharpening.

There, standing near the edge of the parking lot, was a man she didn’t recognize.

He was tall, with dark hair that fell over his eyes in a way that was both rugged and calculated. His broad shoulders and muscular build made him stand out among the students and staff, and there was something about the way he carried himself—something commanding, almost predatory.
Lara’s gaze locked with his for a brief moment. His eyes were a piercing grey, filled with an intensity that sent a shiver down her spine.

But before she could say anything, the man turned and disappeared around the corner of the building.

“Who was that?” Lara asked, more to herself than her friends.

“Who was who?” Kate asked, following her gaze.

“The guy by the parking lot,” Lara said, her heart racing.

Kate frowned. “I didn’t see anyone.”

Lilly shook her head. “Me neither. Are you sure you’re okay, Lara?”

“I’m fine,” Lara said quickly, though her wolf growled softly in the back of her mind.

The Alpha's Presence

Throughout the day, Lara couldn't shake the feeling that she was being watched. Every so often, she'd catch a glimpse of the dark-haired man—standing near the gym, leaning against the library wall, or walking past the cafeteria.

But every time she tried to get closer, he was gone before she could reach him.

By the time school ended, Lara's frustration had reached its peak. She stormed out to the parking lot, scanning the area for any sign of him.

"He's not here," Jessie's voice came from behind her.

Lara spun around, startled. "What are you talking about?"
Jessie leaned against her car; his arms crossed. "The guy you've been chasing all day. He's not here anymore."

"How do you know about that?" Lara asked, narrowing her eyes.

Jessie shrugged. "You're not exactly subtle. I've been keeping an eye on you, just in case."

"In case of what?" Lara asked, crossing her arms.

Jessie's expression darkened. "In case he's who I think he is."

Lara's heart skipped a beat. "And who do you think he is?"
Jessie hesitated, his jaw tightening. "An alpha. A powerful one.

A New Threat

The word hung in the air, heavy with meaning. Lara had heard of alphas before—wolves who were stronger, faster, and more dominant than the rest of their kind. But what would an alpha be doing in Kaiapoi?

"What does he want?" Lara asked, her voice steady despite the unease building inside her.

Jessie shook his head. "I don't know. But if he's been watching you, it's not a coincidence."

Lara's wolf growled in agreement, her instincts warning her of danger.

"Do you think he's a threat?" she asked.

Jessie hesitated, his blue eyes meeting hers. "I don't know. But until we figure out what he wants, you need to be careful."

Lara nodded, determination hardening her resolve. "Then let's figure it out."
Jessie smirked, a hint of admiration in his gaze. "You're not afraid, are you?"

"Should I be?" Lara shot back, raising an eyebrow.

Jessie laughed, shaking his head. "Not bad, wolf-girl. Not bad at all."

Chapter 3: The Shadow in the Woods

Lara couldn't get him out of her head—the man with the piercing grey eyes and commanding presence. Every time she replayed their brief encounters in her mind, her wolf stirred, restless and alert. She didn't know what he wanted or why he was watching her, but she was determined to find out.

Jessie's warning rang in her ears: *"Be careful."* But caution wasn't exactly her strong suit.

Another Day, Another Mystery

The next day at school, Lara found herself scanning the halls, half-expecting to see him leaning against a locker or standing in the shadows of the gym. But as the hours dragged on, there was no sign of him.

Kate and Lilly didn't seem to notice Lara's distraction, though Jessie wasn't so easily fooled.

"You're still thinking about him," he said, falling into step beside her as she walked to her next class.

Lara shot him a sidelong glance. "And if I am?"
Jessie smirked. "I can't decide if you're curious or reckless."

"Maybe both," Lara admitted, adjusting her bag on her shoulder. "You think he's dangerous, don't you?"

"I think anyone who spends their time lurking around high schools is worth keeping an eye on," Jessie said. "Especially if they're an alpha."

Lara frowned. "You keep saying that, like it means something."

Jessie stopped walking, forcing her to turn and face him. "It does mean something. Alphas don't just show up for no reason, Lara. They're territorial, and they're powerful. If he's sniffing around you, it's because he sees something in you that he wants."

Lara swallowed hard, Jessie's words sending a shiver down her spine. "Like what?"

Jessie's expression softened slightly, though his voice remained firm. "That's what we need to figure out."

Training in the Woods

After school, Jessie took Lara back to the woods for another training session. This time, he focused on helping her hone her instincts, pushing her to rely less on brute strength and more on strategy.

"You're bigger than most wolves," Jessie said as they circled each other, his blue eyes sharp. "That's an advantage, but it also makes you a target. Smaller wolves will try to outmanoeuvre you. You have to stay one step ahead."

Lara smirked. "Smaller wolves like you?"

Jessie raised an eyebrow. “Careful, wolf-girl. I’m faster than I look.”
He lunged at her, but Lara was ready this time. She sidestepped his attack, using her momentum to sweep his legs out from under him. Jessie hit the ground with a grunt, and Lara pinned him down, a triumphant grin on her face.

“Faster, huh?” she teased.

Jessie laughed; his blue eyes gleaming with amusement. “Not bad. But you’re not done yet.”
In a flash, he twisted beneath her, flipping her onto her back and pinning her wrists above her head.

“Lesson two,” Jessie said, leaning closer. “Never let your guard down.”

Lara’s breath hitched, her heart pounding in her chest. The air between them felt charged, and for a moment, neither of them moved.

Jessie’s smirk faded, his gaze softening as he looked down at her. “You’re stronger than you realize, Lara,” he said quietly. “But strength isn’t just about fighting. It’s about knowing when to fight—and when to trust someone to have your back.”

Lara’s cheeks flushed, and she quickly looked away. “You’re starting to sound like a fortune cookie.”

Jessie laughed, releasing her wrists and offering her a hand. “Come on. One more round, and then we’re done for today.”

The Alpha Returns

That night, Lara couldn't sleep. Her mind was racing, filled with thoughts of Jessie's words, her training, and the mysterious man who seemed to be watching her every move.

Unable to stay still, she slipped out of the house and made her way to the woods. The moonlight filtered through the trees, casting long shadows across the forest floor.

Her wolf stirred, alert but calm. This was her territory, her sanctuary.
But as she moved deeper into the woods, a familiar scent filled the air—one that made her wolf growl softly in warning.

He was here.

Lara slowed her pace, her senses sharpening as she scanned the shadows. The scent grew stronger, mingling with the cool night air.

"Looking for someone?"

The voice was deep and smooth, sending a shiver down her spine. Lara turned quickly, her heart racing as she came face-to-face with the dark-haired man.

He stood a few feet away; his hands tucked casually into the pockets of his leather jacket. Up close, he was even more striking than she remembered—tall and broad-shouldered, with

sharp features and piercing grey eyes that seemed to see right through her.
“Who are you?” Lara demanded, her voice steady despite the nervous energy coursing through her.

The man tilted his head slightly, a faint smile playing at his lips. “You don’t know?”

Lara growled softly, her wolf pushing to the surface. “I’m not in the mood for games.”

The man chuckled, his voice low and smooth. “Fair enough. My name is Ryker.”

“Why are you here?” Lara asked, her wolf growling louder.

Ryker stepped closer, his movements slow and deliberate. “Because I’ve been looking for you.”

Lara’s heart skipped a beat, but she didn’t back down. “Why?”

Ryker’s smile faded, and his expression grew serious. “Because you’re not like the others. You’re stronger. Bigger. Different. And I want to know why.”

Lara clenched her fists, her wolf bristling with both curiosity and defiance. “Maybe I don’t want to tell you.”

Ryker raised an eyebrow, his gaze locking onto hers. “Then I guess I’ll have to find out for myself.”

Before Lara could respond, Ryker turned and disappeared into the shadows, leaving her alone in the moonlit clearing.

The Question

The next morning, Lara sat in her usual spot at school, her mind racing with questions about Ryker.

"Earth to Lara," Kate said, waving a hand in front of her face. "Are you even listening?"
"Sorry," Lara said quickly. "What were you saying?"

"I was saying you've been acting weird all morning," Kate said, narrowing her eyes. "What's going on?"

Lara hesitated, glancing around to make sure no one was listening. "I think someone's following me," she admitted.

Kate frowned. "Who?"

"A guy," Lara said. "I don't know much about him, but…"

"But what?" Kate prompted.

Lara sighed. "He says he's been looking for me."

Kate's eyes widened. "And you're just telling me this now? Who is he?"
"I don't know," Lara said honestly. "But I'm going to find out."

Chapter 4: The Pull of Shadows

The hum of the school day faded into the background as Lara sat in the library, her thoughts consumed by her encounter with Ryker. His name lingered in her mind like a whispered secret; his piercing grey eyes etched into her memory.

She couldn't deny it: there was something about him that drew her in. It wasn't just his striking looks or the confidence in his every move—it was the way her wolf had reacted to him, a mix of curiosity and something deeper, more primal.

She tried to focus on the history textbook in front of her, but her mind refused to cooperate. What did he mean when he said he'd been looking for her? And why did her wolf stir every time she thought of him?

The sound of a chair scraping across the floor snapped her out of her thoughts. Jessie dropped into the seat across from her, his usual smirk firmly in place.

"You're brooding," he said, resting his arms on the table.
"I'm thinking," Lara corrected, closing her textbook.

"About him?" Jessie asked, his tone sharper than she'd expected.

Lara narrowed her eyes. "Are you spying on me now?"

Jessie shrugged. "You make it hard not to notice when you're distracted. So, what did he say to you?"

Lara hesitated, debating how much to share. "He said he's been looking for me."

Jessie's smirk vanished, replaced by a look of concern. "That's not good."

"What do you mean?"

Jessie leaned closer, lowering his voice. "Alphas don't just wander into town without a reason, and they definitely don't go looking for random wolves. He's after something, Lara. Don't let him fool you."

Lara bristled at his tone. "He hasn't fooled me. I'm just trying to figure out what he wants."
Jessie shook his head. "Be careful, wolf-girl. Guys like him don't play fair."

A Flash of Luxury

After school, Lara walked out to the parking lot, her wolf stirring as a familiar scent filled the air. She turned toward the source, her breath catching as she spotted a sleek black sports car parked near the gate.

Ryker leaned casually against the car, his dark hair catching the sunlight. He looked entirely out of place in Kaiapoi, like a figure from a magazine dropped into the small-town scenery.

Her heart raced as their eyes met. For a moment, the world seemed to fall away, leaving only the magnetic pull between them.

Ryker smirked, his gaze sweeping over her before he opened the car door. “Need a ride?”

Lara hesitated, glancing around. Kate and Lilly were standing nearby, their mouths hanging open as they stared at the car—and its driver.

“Who’s that?” Kate whispered.

“Just… someone I met,” Lara said, her voice uncertain.

“Someone you met?” Kate repeated, her eyes narrowing. “And he just happens to drive *that*?”

Lilly nudged her. “He’s waiting, Lara.”

Lara swallowed hard, her wolf pushing her forward. Before she could think too much about it, she walked over to Ryker’s car.

“Where are we going?” she asked, her voice steady despite the rapid beat of her heart.

Ryker’s smirk widened. “Somewhere we can talk.”

The Pull Between Them

They drove out of town, the car’s engine purring as it sped down the winding road. Lara tried to ignore the way her wolf seemed to

hum with energy in Ryker's presence, a sensation that was both thrilling and unsettling.
"You don't belong in a place like this," Ryker said, breaking the silence.

Lara frowned. "What's that supposed to mean?"

Ryker glanced at her, his grey eyes glinting. "You're too strong, too… unique. You feel it, don't you? That you're different."

Lara's wolf growled softly, torn between pride and caution. "What do you know about me?" she asked.

"Enough to know you're not like the others," Ryker said. "And enough to know you're wasting your potential here."

Lara bristled at his words. "I'm not wasting anything. I'm learning how to control what I can do."

"With Jessie?" Ryker asked, his tone almost mocking.

Lara's jaw tightened. "He's been helping me."

Ryker chuckled, the sound low and rich. "Helping you? Or holding you back?"

Lara turned to face him, her wolf growling louder. "What do you want from me, Ryker?"

Ryker slowed the car, pulling off to the side of the road. He turned to her, his expression serious now. "I want to help you see what you're capable of. You have no idea how powerful you are, Lara. But I do."

The intensity in his gaze made her stomach flip, and for a moment, she was at a loss for words.

Tension in the Air

When Ryker dropped her off back in town, Jessie was waiting.

He was leaning against his truck, his arms crossed and his expression dark. Lara's wolf tensed at the sight of him, sensing the storm brewing between the two men.

"Busy day?" Jessie asked as Lara stepped out of the car.

"Something like that," Lara said, trying to keep her tone neutral.

Ryker stepped out of his car; his movements deliberate as he approached. The air between him and Jessie crackled with tension, their gazes locking like two predators sizing each other up.

"This must be Jessie," Ryker said, his tone cool.

Jessie didn't take his eyes off him. "And you must be the creep hanging around my territory."

Ryker smirked. "Your territory? Last I checked, you're not an alpha."
Jessie stepped forward; his fists clenched. "And last I checked; this wasn't your business."

Lara moved between them, her wolf pushing her to defuse the situation. “Stop it, both of you,” she said firmly.
Jessie’s gaze softened slightly as he looked at her. “Lara, you don’t know who this guy is.”

“And you don’t know what I want,” Ryker countered, his voice steady.

“Maybe not,” Jessie said, his tone low. “But I’m not going to let you mess with her.”

The challenge in his voice was clear, and Ryker’s smirk faded, replaced by a look of cold determination.

“This isn’t over,” Ryker said, his grey eyes flicking to Lara one last time before he turned and walked back to his car.

As the engine roared to life and the sleek black car disappeared down the road, Lara felt the weight of Jessie’s gaze on her.

“What are you doing, Lara?” he asked quietly.

She looked up at him, unsure of how to answer. All she knew was that the pull she felt toward Ryker wasn’t going away—and she didn’t know if she wanted it to.

Chapter 5: A Dance of Shadows

The hum of the school day felt dull to Lara. Nothing seemed to settle her restless energy—not her classes, not her friends' chatter, not even Jessie's constant hovering. Her wolf had been on edge since Ryker's appearance, and the memory of his piercing grey eyes and confident smirk was impossible to shake.

She tried to tell herself it was nothing. Just some strange alpha passing through. But even she didn't believe that.

Her wolf knew better.

The Invitation

It was late afternoon when Lara stepped out of school, the golden light of the sun casting long shadows across the parking lot. Kate and Lilly were already gone, and Jessie had been called away for some family errand, leaving Lara alone for once.

As she walked toward her car, she felt it again—that familiar pull in her chest, a subtle tug that made her stop in her tracks. She turned, and there he was.

Ryker stood leaning against a sleek black sports car, the sunlight glinting off its polished surface. He looked completely at ease; his hands tucked into the pockets of his leather jacket and his sharp grey eyes fixed on her.

Lara's wolf stirred, restless and curious.

"Waiting for someone?" Ryker asked, his voice smooth as silk.

Lara crossed her arms, trying to ignore the way her pulse quickened. "What do you want?"

Ryker pushed off the car, closing the distance between them with easy, confident strides. "I could ask you the same thing. You've been on my mind, Lara."

Her heart skipped a beat, but she quickly masked her reaction. "I don't even know you."
"Not yet," Ryker said with a smirk, his voice dropping slightly. "But something tells me you've felt it too. That pull."

Lara opened her mouth to argue, but the words wouldn't come. She had felt it, as much as she wanted to deny it.

"What do you want, Ryker?" she asked again, her voice quieter this time.

Ryker smiled, his grey eyes softening just enough to unsettle her. "I want to show you something. Come with me."

Her wolf didn't protest. In fact, it seemed eager, pushing her toward him. Against her better judgment, Lara found herself nodding.

The Drive

Ryker opened the passenger door of his car, gesturing for her to get in. Lara hesitated for only a moment before sliding into the seat, the rich leather cool against her skin.
As the car roared to life, she couldn't help but glance at him. Everything about Ryker seemed effortless—the way he handled

the wheel, the quiet confidence in his posture, the faint smirk that never seemed to leave his lips.

“Where are we going?” Lara asked as they sped out of town.

“You’ll see,” Ryker replied, his tone teasing.

The engine purred as they wound through the countryside, the scenery blurring past in streaks of green and gold. For the first time in days, Lara felt herself relax, the tension in her chest easing as the pull toward Ryker deepened.

The View

Ryker finally stopped at the top of a hill overlooking the river. The sun was setting, painting the water in shades of orange and pink. The view was breathtaking, and for a moment, Lara forgot her unease.

“This is beautiful,” she said, stepping out of the car.

Ryker leaned against the hood, his arms crossed as he watched her. “I thought you’d like it.

Lara turned to him, her curiosity getting the better of her. “Why are you doing this?”

“Doing what?” Ryker asked, raising an eyebrow.

“Chasing me,” Lara said bluntly. “You’ve been watching me, following me… Why?”

Ryker’s smirk faded slightly, replaced by something softer, almost vulnerable. “Because you’re different, Lara. Stronger. You don’t even realize what you’re capable of, but I see it.”

Lara's cheeks flushed, and she looked away. "You don't know me."

"Maybe not," Ryker said, stepping closer. "But I know enough to see that you're wasting your time here. With him."
er eyes snapped back to his. "You mean Jessie."

Ryker nodded. "He doesn't understand you—not the way I do. He sees a girl trying to control her power. I see someone who was born to lead."

Lara's breath caught in her throat, her wolf stirring in agreement. She hated how much his words affected her, how they made her feel seen in a way she hadn't before.

"You don't know what you're talking about," she said, but her voice lacked conviction.

Ryker stepped even closer, his presence overwhelming. "Don't I?" The space between them felt charged, the air thick with tension. Ryker reached out, his fingers brushing a strand of hair from her face.

"You feel it, don't you?" he asked, his voice low.

Lara swallowed hard, her heart racing. "I don't know what you're talking about."
Ryker smiled, his hand dropping back to his side. "You will."

The Rescue

The moment was interrupted by a sound in the woods—a low growl that made Lara's wolf snap to attention.

She turned toward the trees, her senses sharpening. "Do you hear that?"

Ryker was already moving, his expression serious. "Stay close."

The growl grew louder, and a rogue wolf stepped out of the shadows, its yellow eyes glowing with malice.

Lara shifted instinctively, her wolf taking over in a flash of power and fur. She stood tall, her golden-brown coat gleaming in the fading light as she squared off against the rogue.

The fight was fast and brutal. The rogue lunged at her, its claws swiping through the air, but Lara was faster. She dodged its attack, her teeth snapping dangerously close to its neck.
But the rogue was relentless, forcing her back with its sheer ferocity.

Before she could recover, Ryker appeared, his own wolf a massive, dark-furred beast with piercing grey eyes. He was larger than any wolf Lara had ever seen, his presence commanding and terrifying.

He attacked the rogue with brutal efficiency, his movements precise and calculated. Within moments, the rogue was defeated, limping back into the shadows with a pained howl.

Ryker shifted back to his human form effortlessly, his expression calm despite the fight. Lara followed suit, her chest heaving as she caught her breath.
“Are you okay?” Ryker asked, stepping closer.

“I… I’m fine,” Lara said, though her body ached from the effort.

Ryker smiled, his hand brushing against hers. “Good. You handled yourself well.”

Lara looked up at him, her wolf still humming with energy. “Thank you. For stepping in.”

“Always,” Ryker said softly, his grey eyes locking onto hers.

The pull between them felt stronger than ever, and for a moment, Lara let herself get lost in it.

Chapter 6: A Bond Unfolding

The woods felt alive in a way they never had before. Every leaf rustled with purpose; every shadow seemed to hold a secret. And at the centre of it all stood Ryker.

Lara's heart was still racing from the fight, her chest rising and falling as she caught her breath. Ryker stood close, his grey eyes steady and unreadable, but the faintest trace of a smile played on his lips.

"You're stronger than you think," he said, his voice low and almost tender.

Lara's wolf bristled with pride at the words, but her human side hesitated. There was something about the way Ryker looked at her, like he saw straight through her walls, past her doubts, and into the part of her she wasn't sure she understood yet.

"Why do they keep coming?" she asked, her voice steady but tinged with frustration. "Why are there so many rogues after me?"

Ryker hesitated, his jaw tightening. It was subtle, but enough for Lara to notice.

"You know something," she pressed, stepping closer. "What is it?"

For a moment, Ryker looked away, as if weighing his words. Then he turned back to her, his gaze softer than she'd ever seen it.

"They're coming because of us," he said finally.

Lara frowned, confusion flickering across her face. “Us?”

Ryker nodded. “You feel it, don’t you? That pull? It’s not just chance, Lara. It’s something bigger—something neither of us can control.”

Her heart skipped a beat. She *had* felt it, ever since the moment their eyes met. It was like a thread connecting them, pulling her toward him no matter how much she tried to resist. There’s a heat in him she couldn’t explain—like every glance, every careless smirk, tugs at something deep inside her, pulling her closer even when she knew in her mind, she should run.
“What does that have to do with the rogues?” she asked.

Ryker took a step closer, his voice lowering. “Because if we’re together—truly together—we’ll be unstoppable. Our bond will make us stronger than any pack that’s ever existed. They’re afraid of what we could become, and they’ll do anything to stop it.”

Lara’s breath caught in her throat. She didn’t know what to say, her mind racing as her wolf stirred in agreement. He stepped a little closer, and it was like her whole body forgot how to breathe—heat curling low in her belly, every nerve alive, craving a touch he hadn’t even given yet.

“And what about you?” she asked finally. “Are you afraid of it?”

Ryker smiled faintly, his hand reaching up to brush a strand of hair from her face. The touch sent a spark through her, her wolf humming in approval.

"Not afraid," he said softly. "But I'm not sure you're ready to face what comes with it."

A Moment of Weakness

Back at her house, Lara couldn't stop thinking about Ryker's words. The idea of their bond terrified her, but it also stirred something deep inside—something she couldn't ignore.

Her wolf wanted him.

She tried to push the thought away, distracting herself with training and schoolwork, but it was no use. The pull was too strong, and the memory of his touch lingered like a ghost. Her wolf paced inside her, wild and wanting, the moment his scent hit her—dark, intoxicating, and threaded with something that made her body ache in places words couldn't reach.

That night, as she lay in bed, she found herself staring at the moonlight streaming through her window. Her necklace glowed faintly against her chest, a steady pulse that mirrored her heartbeat.

Before she could stop herself, she grabbed her phone and texted Ryker.

"I need to talk."

The response came almost immediately.

"Come outside."

The Dance of Wolves

Lara slipped out of the house, her bare feet brushing against the cool grass. Ryker was waiting by the edge of the woods, leaning casually against a tree.

“Couldn’t sleep?” he asked, his tone light but his gaze intense.

“No,” Lara admitted, crossing her arms. “I can’t stop thinking about what you said.”

Ryker nodded, stepping closer. “I figured as much.”
“I don’t understand any of this,” Lara said, her voice rising slightly. “This pull, this… connection. I didn’t ask for it.”

“Neither did I,” Ryker said simply as he gazed deep into her eyes.

The honesty in his voice took her by surprise, and she looked up at him, searching his face for answers.

“But that doesn’t mean it’s not real,” he continued, his voice softening. “I feel it too, Lara. And as much as I tried to stay away, I couldn’t. Something keeps pulling me back to you.”

Her breath hitched, her heart pounding as he stepped even closer. His presence was overwhelming, his scent filling her senses and making her wolf push to the surface.

“And what happens if we give in?” she asked, her voice barely above a whisper.

Ryker's hand came up to cup her face, his thumb brushing lightly against her cheek. The touch sent a shiver down her spine, her wolf practically roaring with approval.

"Then we become unstoppable," he said, his gaze locked onto hers.

For a moment, the world seemed to stand still. The air between them was electric, charged with a tension that was impossible to ignore. Lara's wolf urged her forward, and for once, she didn't fight it.

She closed the distance between them, her lips brushing against his in a tentative kiss.

Ryker responded immediately, his arms wrapping around her as he deepened the kiss. The intensity of it took her breath away, her body pressing against his as the pull between them grew stronger.

It was like nothing she'd ever felt before—raw, overwhelming, and impossible to resist.

Interrupted

The moment was broken by the sound of footsteps in the distance. Ryker pulled back; his expression sharp as his wolf rose to the surface.

"Someone's coming," he said, his voice low.

Lara turned toward the sound, her senses sharpening as her wolf pushed to the forefront. A familiar scent filled the air, and her heart sank.

"Jessie," she said quietly.

Ryker's expression darkened, but he didn't move. Jessie appeared moments later, his blue eyes narrowing as he took in the scene.

"What's going on here?" Jessie asked, his tone clipped.

"Nothing that concerns you," Ryker said smoothly, his hand brushing lightly against Lara's arm.

Jessie's gaze flicked to Ryker's hand, and his jaw tightened. "It does concern me if you're messing with her."

"I'm not messing with anyone," Ryker said, his voice calm but laced with challenge. "Lara knows exactly what she wants."

Jessie looked at Lara, his expression softening slightly. "Lara, is that true?"

Lara opened her mouth to respond, but the words wouldn't come. She didn't know what to say, torn between the pull she felt toward Ryker and the loyalty she felt toward Jessie.

"She doesn't owe you an explanation," Ryker said, stepping in front of her.
Jessie's fists clenched, his wolf bristling with anger. "I don't trust you."

“You don’t have to,” Ryker replied. “But if you want what’s best for her, you’ll step aside.”

The tension between them crackled like a storm, but before either could make a move, Lara stepped between them.

“Stop it,” she said firmly. “This isn’t helping.”

Jessie hesitated, his gaze lingering on her for a moment before he nodded. “Fine. But this isn’t over.”

As Jessie disappeared into the woods, Ryker turned to Lara, his expression softening.

“You don’t have to choose now,” he said quietly. “But when you’re ready, you’ll know where to find me.”

He stepped back into the shadows, leaving Lara alone under the moonlight, her heart torn and her wolf restless.

Chapter 7: The Heart's Divide

The night air felt heavy as Lara stood at the edge of the woods, her thoughts spinning. Ryker's words echoed in her mind, his touch still lingering on her skin. *"When you're ready, you'll know where to find me."*

But then there was Jessie—steady, familiar, and always ready to stand by her side. Her loyalty to him felt natural, but the pull she felt toward Ryker was undeniable, something deeper than instinct, something that made her wolf burn with a fierce, uncontrollable energy.

She didn't know what scared her more—her growing feelings for Ryker or the fact that a part of her didn't want to fight them.

A Conversation with Jessie

The next morning, Jessie was waiting for her outside her house, leaning against his truck. His blue eyes held a mix of frustration and concern, and Lara braced herself for the conversation she knew was coming.

"Morning," Jessie said, his tone casual but tense.
"Morning," Lara replied, forcing a smile as she stepped outside.

Jessie pushed off the truck, falling into step beside her as they walked toward the woods. "I wanted to talk about last night."

Lara sighed, shoving her hands into her jacket pockets. "Jessie, I—""I'm worried about you," Jessie interrupted, his voice firm.

“That guy—Ryker—he’s dangerous, Lara. You don’t know anything about him.”

“I know enough,” Lara said, her tone sharper than she intended.

Jessie stopped walking, his gaze narrowing. “Do you? Because from where I’m standing, it looks like he’s messing with your head.”

Lara turned to face him, her wolf stirring defensively. “You don’t understand, Jessie. There’s something between us—something I can’t explain.”

“Lara,” Jessie said, his voice softening, “I’ve known you my whole life. I’ve seen you fight, grow, and figure out who you are. And now this guy shows up, and suddenly you’re ready to throw all of that away?”

“I’m not throwing anything away,” Lara said, her voice rising. “But what I feel for him—it’s not something I can ignore.”

Jessie’s expression hardened, his fists clenching at his sides. “You don’t have to ignore it. But you should question it.”

Before Lara could respond, Jessie shook his head and turned back toward his truck. “Just… be careful, okay? I don’t want to see you get hurt.”

Lara watched him drive away, her chest aching with a mix of guilt and frustration.

The Pull Grows Stronger

That evening, Lara couldn't shake the restless energy coursing through her. She tried to focus on anything else—training, homework, even texting Kate and Lilly—but nothing helped. The pull toward Ryker was stronger than ever, an insistent hum that wouldn't leave her alone.

Finally, she gave in.

Lara stepped outside and shifted, her wolf taking over as she ran toward the hill where Ryker had taken her before. The cool night air rushed past her, the thrill of the run soothing her nerves as her paws pounded against the earth.

When she reached the hilltop, he was already there.

Ryker leaned against his car, his dark jacket blending into the shadows. His grey eyes lit up when he saw her, and a slow smile spread across his face.

"I was wondering when you'd come back," he said, his voice low and teasing.

Lara shifted back to her human form, standing a few feet away from him. "I couldn't stay away."

Ryker's smile widened, and he stepped closer, his gaze holding hers. "Neither could I."

The tension between them was electric, the pull undeniable. Ryker reached out, his fingers brushing against her cheek.

"You feel it too, don't you?" he asked softly.

Lara nodded, her wolf growling in approval. "I don't know what to do with it."

"Don't fight it," Ryker said, his voice dropping. "Just let it happen."

A Moment of Vulnerability

Lara closed the distance between them, her breath hitching as Ryker's hands settled on her hips. His touch was firm but gentle, his presence overwhelming in the best way.

For a moment, she let herself get lost in it—the warmth of his hands, the intensity of his gaze, the way her wolf seemed to melt under his touch.

"I don't know what's happening to me," she admitted, her voice barely above a whisper.

Ryker's expression softened, and he leaned closer, his forehead resting against hers. "You're becoming who you were meant to be. And you don't have to do it alone."

Lara's heart pounded as his lips brushed against hers, the kiss slow and tentative at first. But as the pull between them grew stronger, so did the intensity. Her fingers tangled in his jacket, pulling him closer as her wolf howled with approval.

When they finally pulled apart, Ryker's gray eyes searched hers, his voice soft but firm. "You're mine, Lara. You always have been."

The words sent a shiver down her spine, but before she could respond, her wolf growled in warning.

The Threat Grows

A sharp howl echoed through the woods, breaking the moment. Lara stiffened, her senses sharpening as the scent of rogues filled the air.

Ryker shifted immediately, his massive black wolf standing protectively in front of her. Lara followed suit, her golden-brown wolf bristling with anticipation.

The rogues emerged from the shadows; their glowing yellow eyes filled with malice. There were at least four of them, circling slowly as they growled and snapped.

Ryker growled low in his throat, his posture commanding and confident. The rogues hesitated, clearly intimidated, but they didn't retreat.

"Stay close," Ryker said through their mind-link, his voice steady and sure.

Lara crouched low; her wolf ready to fight. The pull between her and Ryker burned brighter than ever, their instincts aligning in a way that felt natural, almost inevitable.

When the rogues attacked, they moved as one.

Lara and Ryker fought side by side, their movements fluid and precise. Her wolf was stronger and faster than she'd ever felt before, the bond between them amplifying her abilities in ways she couldn't explain.

The fight was brutal, but the rogues didn't stand a chance.

As the last one fled into the shadows, Lara shifted back, her body trembling with adrenaline. Ryker followed, his hand reaching out to steady her.

"You're incredible," he said, his voice filled with awe.

Lara looked up at him, her breath catching at the intensity in his gaze. "I couldn't have done it without you."

"You could've," Ryker said with a small smile. "But I'm glad I was here."

For a moment, they stood in silence, the bond between them stronger than ever. Lara knew the road ahead wouldn't be easy, but as she looked into Ryker's eyes, she felt something she hadn't in a long time.

Hope.

Chapter 8: The Promise of Forever

The woods had gone silent after the fight with the rogues, but the air between Lara and Ryker was anything but calm.

They walked side by side back to her house, their steps slow and deliberate. Neither of them spoke, but Lara could feel the unspoken words lingering between them, heavier with every passing moment.

When they reached her back porch, Ryker stopped and turned to her. His gray eyes were unreadable, but there was a softness in his expression that made her heart ache.

“You fought well tonight,” he said quietly.

“Thanks,” Lara replied, brushing a stray leaf out of her hair. “I guess the training is paying off.”

“It’s more than that,” Ryker said, his gaze steady. “You’re getting stronger, Lara. And it’s not just from the fights. It’s… us.”

Lara’s breath caught, and her wolf stirred in agreement. “What do you mean?”

Ryker hesitated for a moment, as if searching for the right words. “The bond between us—it’s not just a feeling. It’s something real, something powerful. And as we get closer, it’s making you stronger.”

Lara frowned; her curiosity piqued. “Why? How does it work?”

Ryker stepped closer, his hand brushing against hers. The simple touch sent a shiver through her, her wolf humming with approval.

"Alphas like us," he began, his voice low, "are connected in ways others can't understand. When two mates find each other, the bond creates a link between them—a connection that's physical, emotional, and mental."

"A mind-link," Lara said, the words coming to her unbidden.

Ryker nodded. "Exactly. It's not fully there yet, but you've felt it, haven't you? That sense of knowing what I'm thinking, what I'm feeling?"

Lara thought back to their fights, their shared glances, the way she always seemed to know where he was. She had thought it was instinct, but now it made sense.

"It'll get stronger," Ryker continued, his voice softer now. "Especially once we're… fully bonded."

The meaning behind his words was clear, and Lara's cheeks flushed. "You mean once we…"

Ryker smiled faintly. "Married first, though. I'm not an animal, Lara."

She laughed despite herself, the tension easing for a moment. But as she looked up at him, her heart raced. The pull between them was undeniable, and her wolf urged her forward.

"I should go inside," she said quietly, stepping toward the door.

Ryker caught her hand, stopping her. "Not yet," he said, his voice low and filled with meaning. "Let me take you out. Tomorrow night."

"Like… a date?" Lara asked, her pulse quickening.

Ryker nodded, his smirk returning. "Call it whatever you want. But say yes."

Lara hesitated for only a moment before nodding. "Okay."

The First Date

The following evening, Ryker picked her up in his sleek black car, the same one that had drawn every eye in the school parking lot. Lara felt a nervous flutter in her stomach as she climbed in, her wolf unusually quiet but content.

"Where are we going?" she asked as they sped out of town.

"You'll see," Ryker replied, his tone teasing.

They drove for nearly an hour, the countryside giving way to the lights of a nearby city. Ryker parked in front of an elegant restaurant, its modern design and soft golden lighting exuding sophistication.

"This place looks expensive," Lara said as they stepped inside. Ryker shrugged, his hand resting lightly on the small of her back. "Nothing's too good for you."

The words sent a shiver down her spine, and she tried to ignore the way her heart fluttered.

The dinner was perfect—delicious food, soft music, and Ryker's steady gaze holding hers across the table. They talked about everything and nothing, and for the first time, Lara let herself relax in his presence.

"Tell me something about you," she said, resting her chin on her hand. "Something no one else knows."

Ryker's smirk faded, replaced by a thoughtful expression. "I've never done this before," he admitted.

"Done what?"
"Found someone like you," Ryker said, his voice soft but sure. "Someone who makes me want to stay in one place. Who makes me feel… complete."

Lara's cheeks flushed, but she didn't look away. "I've never done this either," she said quietly.

"Then we're figuring it out together," Ryker said, his hand brushing against hers.

The Proposal

Over the next few weeks, Lara and Ryker grew closer. He took her on more dates—picnics by the river, walks through the woods, even an impromptu dance under the stars.

With every moment they spent together, the bond between them grew stronger. Lara felt it in the way her wolf seemed calmer around him, the way her strength increased during training, and the way her heart raced every time he looked at her.

But the nights weren't always peaceful. The rogues were growing bolder, their attacks more frequent and coordinated. It was clear they were running out of time.

One night, after a particularly brutal fight, Ryker led her to the hilltop where they'd shared their first kiss. The moonlight bathed the landscape in silver, and the air was cool and still.

Ryker turned to face her; his expression serious. "Lara, there's something I need to ask you."

Her heart skipped a beat as he reached into his pocket and pulled out a small velvet box.

"I've been waiting for this moment my whole life," Ryker said, his voice steady but filled with emotion. "I didn't know it until I met you, but you're everything I've ever wanted. You're strong, fearless, and you make me want to be better every day."

Lara's breath caught as he dropped to one knee, opening the box to reveal a stunning ring—a silver band set with a deep blue stone that seemed to shimmer like moonlight.

"Lara," Ryker said, his grey eyes locking onto hers. "Will you marry me?"

Tears filled her eyes, and she nodded, her voice trembling as she said, “Yes.”

Ryker stood, slipping the ring onto her finger before pulling her into a deep, passionate kiss. Every gasp she stifled only seemed to fuel him: his mouth trailed from her lips to the soft curve of her jaw, teeth grazing skin before returning to claim her mouth in a fierce, intoxicating rhythm. Her wolf howled with joy, and for the first time, Lara felt truly whole.

But as the bond between them strengthened, Lara knew their journey was just beginning.

Chapter 9: A Year to Remember

The weeks leading up to graduation were a blur of excitement, planning, and anticipation. Lara had never been so busy—or so happy. Between finishing school and preparing for her wedding to Ryker, her days were full of endless possibilities.

But as graduation day arrived, a shadow of unease crept into her otherwise perfect moment, sparked by her parents' strange behaviour. Her father, normally a quiet but supportive presence, had become more withdrawn. Her mother's smiles didn't quite reach her eyes.

She couldn't shake the feeling that they were holding something back—something important.

Graduation Day

The amphitheatre was buzzing with excitement as Lara joined her classmates in their caps and gowns. The sun shone brightly over the mountains, casting a golden glow over the ceremony.
Lara sat between Kate and Lilly, the three of them stealing glances at Ryker, who stood at the edge of the crowd. He looked impossibly handsome in his tailored suit, his presence drawing whispers from everyone around him.

"Your fiancé is causing quite the distraction," Kate teased, nudging Lara.

Lara grinned, her cheeks flushing. "I can't help it if he's good-looking."

"He's more than good-looking," Lilly added with a laugh. "Half the girls here are swooning, and he hasn't even said a word."

Lara's wolf stirred with satisfaction, a soft growl of approval echoing in her mind.

The Ceremony

Walking across the stage to receive her diploma felt surreal. The crowd cheered, her friends shouted her name, and she couldn't help but glance toward Ryker. His slow, deliberate applause and the proud smirk on his face sent warmth flooding through her.

This was her moment, and Ryker was part of it.

A Father's Secret

The graduation party was still in full swing when Lara stepped outside for some air. The night was cool and quiet, the music from the hall fading into the background. She leaned against the railing, letting the stillness settle over her.

"Big day."

Lara turned to see her father standing a few feet away, his hands in his pockets.

"Yeah," she said softly. "It feels… big."

Her dad nodded, stepping closer. His expression was serious, his gaze heavy with something she couldn't quite place.

"There's something I need to tell you, Lara," he said, his voice steady but tense.

Lara frowned, her wolf stirring uneasily. "What is it?"

Her father hesitated, his jaw tightening. "It's about your nana. About our family."

Lara's heart skipped a beat. "What about her?"

"You've always known you were special," her dad began, his voice dropping. "But what you don't know is why. Your nana wasn't just a wolf, Lara. She came from a bloodline that carried… something more."

"Something more?" Lara echoed, her fingers brushing against her necklace.
Her dad nodded. "Your nana's bloodline holds a kind of power. It's what made her different—what made her stronger. And it's in you too."

Lara's breath caught, her wolf bristling. "Why didn't you tell me this before?"

"Because we hoped it wouldn't matter," her dad admitted, his voice laced with regret. "But now that you're with Ryker, that power is waking up. And if you're not careful, it could destroy you both."
"Destroy us?" Lara whispered, her chest tightening.
Her father nodded. "When two wolves like you and Ryker bond, it amplifies everything—your strength, your abilities, and… your

risks. Your nana tried to control it, but it almost destroyed her. I don't want to see that happen to you."

Lara's mind raced, her wolf growling in confusion and frustration. "Why didn't you tell me this before?"

"Because we didn't think it would come to this," her father said. "But now that you've chosen Ryker, you need to know the truth."

A Friend's Advice

The next morning, Lara found herself walking to Jessie's house, her thoughts swirling. She needed someone to talk to—someone who wasn't directly involved.

Jessie answered the door, his blue eyes lighting up in surprise. "Lara? Everything okay?"

"Can I come in?" she asked, her voice quieter than usual.

"Of course," Jessie said, stepping aside.

They sat on the couch, Jessie watching her carefully as she explained everything her father had told her.

When she finished, Jessie leaned back, his expression thoughtful. "That's… a lot to take in."

"Tell me about it," Lara muttered, running a hand through her hair.

Jessie frowned. "Do you trust Ryker?"

The question caught her off guard. "Of course I do. This isn't about him—it's about me. What if my dad's right? What if this bond is too much for us to handle?"

Jessie hesitated before replying. "Look, I'm not Ryker's biggest fan. But I've seen the way he looks at you, Lara. He's not going anywhere. And if anyone can handle this, it's you."

Lara looked at him, her chest tightening. "You really think so?"

Jessie smiled faintly. "I know so. You're the strongest person I know, Lara. And if Ryker's worth anything, he'll stick by you through this."

Confiding in Ryker

That evening, Lara met Ryker at the clearing where they'd first kissed. The moonlight bathed the landscape in silver, casting a soft glow over the trees.

Ryker leaned against his car, his expression softening as she approached. "You look worried," he said, his voice gentle.

Lara took a deep breath, her wolf urging her to trust him. "I need to talk to you."

"Anything," Ryker said, stepping closer.
Lara told him everything—her father's warning, the power in her bloodline, the risks their bond might bring. As she spoke, Ryker listened intently, his grey eyes steady and unwavering.

When she finished, Ryker reached out, his hands resting on her shoulders.
"Lara," he said softly, "do you trust me?"

"Yes," she said without hesitation.

"Then trust that we can handle this—together," Ryker said, his voice firm. "I don't care how strong this bond gets or what risks it brings. You're worth it. Every part of you."

Tears filled Lara's eyes, and she nodded, her wolf calming at his words. "I don't want to lose you," she whispered.

"You won't," Ryker promised, pulling her into his arms. "I'm not going anywhere."

As they stood together under the moonlight, Lara felt a renewed sense of determination. Whatever challenges lay ahead, she knew one thing for certain: she wouldn't face them alone.

Chapter 10: Forever Begins Tonight

The wedding day arrived in a golden haze, the morning sunlight spilling over the clearing where Lara and Ryker would soon exchange vows. The space had been transformed into something out of a dream: wildflowers lined the aisle, their soft scents mingling with the crisp mountain air, and fairy lights twinkled between the towering trees, casting a warm, magical glow over everything.

Lara stood in the small cabin with Kate and Lilly, the two of them fussing over her dress and veil as her stomach churned with anticipation. Her gown was elegant and simple, its delicate lace hugging her figure before spilling into a soft train. A silver chain around her neck held her glowing crescent moon necklace, its faint pulse mirroring the rhythm of her heart.

"You look incredible," Kate said, her eyes shining as she adjusted Lara's veil.

"Absolutely stunning," Lilly added, grinning. "Ryker is going to lose it when he sees you."

Lara laughed nervously, though her cheeks flushed at the thought. "You think so?"
Kate rolled her eyes. "Lara, the man worships the ground you walk on. Trust me, he's going to lose his mind."

The Walk Down the Aisle

As the music began, Lara stood at the edge of the clearing, her hand gripping her father's arm.

"You ready for this?" her dad asked, his voice soft.

Lara nodded, her heart pounding. "More than ever."

When they stepped onto the aisle, every head turned toward her. Gasps rippled through the crowd, but Lara only had eyes for Ryker.

He stood at the end of the aisle, his tall frame commanding in a tailored black suit that fit him perfectly. His dark hair caught the light, and his piercing grey eyes burned with a raw intensity that sent heat flooding through her.

As their eyes met, everything else faded away. Ryker's expression was unreadable, but the tension in his jaw and the way his hands clenched at his sides told her everything. He wanted her—needed her—and the hunger in his gaze made her wolf stir with excitement.

When she reached him, Ryker extended his hand, his touch warm and steady as he guided her to stand before him.

"You look… breathtaking," he murmured, his voice low and rough.

"Thank you," Lara whispered, her cheeks flushing.

The Ceremony

The officiant began the ceremony, but Lara barely heard the words. Her senses were consumed by Ryker: the heat of his body, the way his thumb brushed against her knuckles, the steady rise and fall of his chest as he breathed.

When it came time to exchange vows, Ryker's voice was steady, though his gaze burned with unspoken emotion.

"Lara," he said, slipping the silver band onto her finger. "You are my mate, my partner, my equal. You make me stronger every day, and I promise to stand by your side, no matter what comes. You're mine, and I'm yours. Always."

Lara's voice trembled as she slid the matching band onto his finger. "Ryker, you've shown me a love I never thought I'd find. You make me brave; you make me whole, and I promise to be by your side for as long as we live. You're mine, and I'm yours. Forever."

When the officiant declared them husband and wife, Ryker wasted no time. His hands cupped her face as he kissed her deeply, his lips claiming hers with a hunger that left her breathless. The crowd erupted into cheers, but Lara barely noticed, her body pressed against his as their bond surged with power. Her lips parted under his, and she tasted that urgent heat—tongues sliding together in a slow, deliberate dance that left her breathless and trembling at the seams.

The Reception

The reception was held in a clearing nearby, where long tables decorated with candles and wildflowers stretched under the canopy of trees. Music filled the air, and the soft glow of the fairy lights made everything feel intimate and magical.

Lara and Ryker moved through the crowd, accepting congratulations and well-wishes from friends and family. But no matter how many people surrounded them, Ryker's attention never wavered. His hand stayed firmly on her waist, his touch possessive yet gentle.
When it came time for their first dance, Ryker led her to the centre of the clearing. The music was slow and romantic, and as he pulled her into his arms, Lara felt the rest of the world fall away.

"You're incredible," Ryker murmured, his lips brushing against her ear.

"You're not so bad yourself," Lara teased, though her breath hitched as his hand slid lower on her back.

Ryker chuckled softly, his grey eyes darkening. "I can't wait to get you alone."

Heat flooded her cheeks, and she looked away, though her wolf howled in agreement.

The Wedding Night

As the night wore on, Lara felt the tension between her and Ryker grow. Every glance, every touch, every shared smile seemed to set her nerves alight. By the time they slipped away from the reception, her body was buzzing with anticipation. Her heart thundered louder than the distant storm, each breath a tremor she couldn't tame.

They returned to Ryker's estate, where the house was quiet and dimly lit. He led her up the sweeping staircase to their room, his hand warm and firm around hers.

When they reached the door, Ryker paused, turning to face her.

"Are you nervous?" he asked, his voice low and intimate.

"A little," Lara admitted, her cheeks flushing.

Ryker stepped closer, his hands settling on her waist as his gaze searched hers. "You don't have to be. I'll take care of you, Lara. Always."

Her breath caught as his lips brushed against hers, the kiss slow and deliberate. Their lips meeting again—slow, curious—like two explorers charting a territory she held in her trembling fingertips. His hands moved to her back, pulling her closer as his mouth claimed hers with growing intensity.

Ryker's lips curved into a wicked smile, and he lifted her effortlessly into his arms, carrying her into the room and kicking the door shut behind them.

Lara's hands tangled in his hair, her body pressing against his as her wolf howled with need. The cool silk sheets whispered against her heated hip as he drew her closer, anchoring her in this shared moment.

"Ryker," she whispered, her voice trembling.

He pulled back just enough to look at her, his grey eyes blazing. "Tell me what you want, my love."

"You," Lara said without hesitation, her heart pounding.

The room was bathed in the soft glow of moonlight, but Lara barely noticed. Her focus was entirely on Ryker—the heat of his hands, the way his breath brushed against her skin, the sheer intensity of his presence.

His fingers traced the hollow of her collarbone, igniting sparks that chased away every lingering doubt.

"You're mine, Lara," Ryker murmured, his voice rough with desire.

"And you're mine," Lara replied, her voice steady despite the whirlwind of emotions surging through her.

Ryker's lips captured hers again, his kisses deep and consuming. His hands explored her body with reverence and hunger, leaving her breathless and trembling beneath his touch.

As his lips trailed down her neck, Lara's wolf growled in approval, her instincts urging her forward. She arched against him, her hands pulling him closer, the bond between them crackling with energy.

Just as Ryker's hands slipped to the hem of her dress, his voice dropped to a low, commanding growl. "Lara, are you ready?" Her heart raced as she looked up at him, her eyes locking onto his. "Yes."

She closed her eyes, surrendering to the swell of sensation—fear and longing melding into one exquisite pulse.

He traced tiny circles over the swell of her breast, each fingertip sending ripples of heat through her core until she ached to feel him closer. Their breaths mingled, soft and ragged, as he pressed his mouth to the curve of her neck, leaving a trail of fire in his wake. She arched into his hand, the slick press of her skin against his palm coaxing a low, hungry groan from deep in his chest. His lips found the sensitive hollow just below her ear, and she bit back a gasp as his tongue teased her with feather-light strokes. A shiver rolled through her when he brushed the smooth valley between her thighs, his touch both teasing and possessive. She tilted her hips, silently begging him for more, and he answered by slipping his hand beneath the fabric of her underwear, warm and insistent.

Every brush of his skin against hers felt electric, as if they were two magnets pulled taut by desire's cruel gravity. When his mouth descended again—kiss deepening into something urgent—she surrendered entirely, her body moulding to his in a delicious give and take.

Chapter 11: A Bond Consummated

Ryker's question lingered in the air, his grey eyes searching hers with a mix of hunger and tenderness.

"Lara are you ready?" he asked again, his voice low, rough, and full of promise.

"Yes," she whispered, her heart pounding in her chest. "I'm ready."

A slow smile spread across Ryker's lips, his gaze darkening with desire. He pulled her closer, their bodies flush as his hands settled on her waist. His lips captured hers again, the kiss deep and consuming. His palm flattened against her back, guiding her into him as heat pooled low and her breath hitched around the delicious weight of his body.

She felt the tremor in his chest against her ear, each pulse syncing with the quickening thrum between her legs.

The soft glow of moonlight filtered through the room, casting long shadows across the walls. Lara felt herself melt into Ryker's touch as his hands moved over her, tracing every curve with deliberate care.
"You're so beautiful," he murmured against her skin, his voice filled with reverence. She tasted him—salt and promise—on the tip of her tongue as his mouth trailed downward, worshipping every inch of her skin.

Lara's breath hitched as his lips trailed down her neck, his kisses sending shivers through her. Her wolf hummed with approval, the bond between them crackling with energy as Ryker's touch became more insistent.

Her fingers tangled in his dark hair, pulling him closer as his hands slipped to the small of her back. Ryker's lips found hers again, the kiss filled with a hunger that left her trembling.

"Ryker," she whispered, her voice barely audible.

He pulled back just enough to look at her, his grey eyes blazing. "You're mine, Lara," he said, his voice firm but full of emotion.

"And you're mine," Lara replied, her voice steady despite the whirlwind of emotions coursing through her.

Ryker lifted her effortlessly, carrying her to the bed and laying her down gently. His hands skimmed over her body, slow and deliberate, as if memorizing every inch of her.

Lara arched into his touch, her breath coming in soft gasps as his lips explored her skin. She felt the bond between them growing stronger with every kiss, every caress, their connection becoming something tangible, almost electric.

"You're perfect," Ryker said, his voice rough as his lips brushed against her collarbone.

"So are you," Lara replied, her hands trailing down his back, feeling the taut muscles beneath his skin.
Their movements became slower, more deliberate, each touch filled with meaning. Ryker's kisses deepened, his hands guiding her as they explored the boundaries of their bond. Lara's wolf

surged forward, her instincts taking over as she clung to him, their connection unlike anything she'd ever experienced.
The world outside disappeared, leaving only the two of them. Their breaths mingled, their hearts beat in unison, and their bond finally solidified in a way that was undeniable. She arched and rolled into him, the slick press of her skin against his palm guiding his every move in a silent, ardent duet. When he finally lifted his head, their eyes locked—dark, heavy-lidded, and full of that raw hunger that set her entire body alight.

When they finally came together, the sensation was overwhelming—a perfect blend of love, passion, and power that left Lara trembling in Ryker's arms. Her wolf howled in her mind; its voice filled with triumph and satisfaction.

Ryker held her close, his lips brushing against her forehead as they lay entwined. "I love you, Lara," he whispered, his voice soft but sure.

"I love you too," Lara replied, her voice thick with emotion.

The Morning After

Lara woke to the soft light of dawn streaming through the window. Ryker's arm was draped over her waist, his warmth a comforting presence beside her. She turned to look at him, her heart swelling at the sight of his peaceful expression.

But as she moved, a strange sensation coursed through her—an unfamiliar energy that made her wolf stir with excitement.
Lara slipped out of bed, careful not to wake Ryker, and stepped in front of the mirror. Her breath caught in her throat as she saw the

faint shimmer of light surrounding her skin, a glow that hadn't been there before.

Her wolf growled softly in her mind, its voice deeper and more powerful than she remembered.

"Lara?" Ryker's voice came from behind her, still thick with sleep.

She turned to see him sitting up, his grey eyes widening as he took her in. "You're glowing," he said, his voice filled with awe.

"So are you," Lara replied, her gaze locking onto him.

Ryker stood, the morning light illuminating his figure. He seemed taller, broader, and more imposing than ever, his dark hair tousled and his eyes sharper than she'd ever seen them.

"What's happening to us?" Lara asked, her voice trembling.

"The bond," Ryker said, stepping closer. "It's changing us."

The Run

Later that morning, Lara and Ryker ventured into the forest. The trees stretched tall and proud around them, the scent of earth and pine filling the air. "I need to shift," Lara said, her wolf restless beneath her skin. Ryker nodded. "Let's do it together." They stood side by side, their bond humming with energy as they let their wolves take over.

Lara's shift was instantaneous, her body transforming in a flash of light. When she opened her eyes, she gasped at the sight of her reflection in the still waters of a nearby stream.

Her wolf was white—pure, brilliant, and shimmering with an almost otherworldly glow. Her coat caught the sunlight, creating a halo of light around her.

Ryker shifted beside her, his wolf larger and darker than ever. His coat was pitch black, his muscles rippling as he moved with quiet confidence. He stood taller than before, his presence commanding and powerful.

They looked at each other, their wolves growling softly in recognition.

"You're stunning," Ryker said through their mind-link, his voice filled with admiration.

"So are you," Lara replied, her wolf's voice steady and sure.

They began to run, their movements perfectly in sync as they weaved through the forest. Lara felt her strength growing with every step, her senses sharper and her body faster than ever before.

Ryker ran beside her, his black wolf a shadow to her light. Together, they were unstoppable—a perfect balance of power and grace.
As they reached the edge of the forest, Ryker slowed, his massive form towering over her as he nudged her gently with his muzzle. Lara's wolf growled softly in approval, their bond pulsing with energy as they stood together.

Whatever challenges lay ahead, Lara knew one thing for certain: she and Ryker were stronger together than they'd ever been apart.

And this was only the beginning.

Chapter 12: A Life Together

The mansion felt like a dream. Its towering stone walls, sprawling grounds, and elegant furnishings seemed like something out of a movie. Yet it was now Lara's home—a place where she and Ryker would begin their new life together as leaders of the pack.

Lara stood at the base of the grand staircase, her hand tracing the smooth banister as she took it all in. The enormity of what lay ahead hit her with a mix of excitement and nerves.

"This is all ours?" she asked, glancing over her shoulder at Ryker.

He leaned casually against the doorway, his dark hair falling over his sharp grey eyes. "It's yours now, too," he said, his voice rich and commanding.

Her wolf stirred at his words, growling softly with satisfaction.

Ryker stepped closer, his presence commanding yet comforting. He reached out, his fingers brushing her cheek. "You're not just my mate, Lara. You're my equal. This pack is as much yours as it is mine."

Lara's heart swelled, and she nodded. "Then let's meet them."

Meeting the Pack

The pack had gathered in the expansive main hall, their excitement palpable as Lara and Ryker entered. Conversations hushed, and all eyes turned toward them.
Lara's wolf bristled with both pride and anticipation as she stood beside Ryker, his hand resting possessively on her lower back.

"This is Lara," Ryker announced, his voice steady and strong. "My mate. Your new alpha."

A ripple of murmurs swept through the crowd, but it wasn't one of dissent—it was awe. The pack instinctively knew that Lara wasn't ordinary. Her white wolf and the glowing energy that surrounded her commanded respect and admiration.

One by one, pack members approached to introduce themselves. Some were formal, offering bows of deference, while others were warm and welcoming. Lara met each one with confidence, though she leaned into Ryker's reassuring touch when the weight of her new role began to feel overwhelming.

"She's perfect," one of the older pack members whispered to another, her voice filled with approval. "Look at her—they're going to lead us into greatness."

A Visit from Friends

A few days later, Kate and Lilly arrived at the mansion for a visit. Lara greeted them at the door, pulling them into a tight hug as they gasped at their surroundings.

"Lara, this place is insane," Kate said, her eyes wide as she took in the grand foyer.

"It's a castle," Lilly added, spinning around to take in the high ceilings and ornate chandeliers. "I can't believe you live here now."

Lara laughed, guiding them into the sitting room where a fire crackled in the hearth. "It's a bit overwhelming, but it's starting to feel like home."

"And how's Ryker?" Kate asked, wiggling her eyebrows.

"He's… amazing," Lara said, her cheeks flushing.

"I'll bet he is," Lilly teased, nudging her.

Their laughter filled the room, and for a moment, Lara felt like everything was falling into place.

Moments of Desire

Later that evening, after Kate and Lilly had gone to bed in one of the mansion's guest suites, Lara found herself standing on the balcony outside her room. The cool night air brushed against her skin, the moon casting a silver glow over the forest below.

She didn't hear Ryker approach, but she felt him—the steady hum of their bond alerting her to his presence.

"You've been busy today," he said, his voice low and rough as he wrapped his arms around her waist.

"So have you," Lara replied, leaning back against his chest.

Ryker nuzzled her neck, his breath hot against her skin. "And yet, all I've been thinking about is you."

Lara's pulse quickened as his hands moved over her hips, his touch firm and possessive.

"Ryker," she whispered, her voice trembling with both desire and anticipation.

"Say my name again," he growled, his teeth grazing the sensitive spot just below her ear.

Lara's knees weakened, but Ryker held her steady, his dominance unmistakable as he turned her to face him. His grey eyes burned with a fierce intensity, and his lips captured hers in a kiss that was both demanding and tender.

He lifted her effortlessly, carrying her inside and laying her down on the bed. His hands explored her body with reverence, his touch igniting a fire that left her trembling beneath him.

"You're mine, Lara," he murmured against her skin, his voice filled with both love and authority.
"And you're mine," Lara replied, her voice steady despite the whirlwind of emotions coursing through her.

The night stretched on, filled with whispered promises, soft moans, and the undeniable pull of their bond. Ryker's dominance was tempered by his tenderness, and Lara surrendered to him completely, her wolf purring with satisfaction.

A Magical Transformation

The next morning, Lara woke to the soft glow of sunlight streaming through the windows. Ryker was already awake, lying beside her with a faint smirk on his lips.

"Good morning, Mrs. Ryker," he teased, his voice rich and playful.

Lara laughed, playfully swatting his chest. "Good morning."

They spent a lazy morning in bed before deciding to go for a run in the forest. The fresh air was invigorating, and Lara's wolf itched to stretch its legs.

When they shifted, Lara's transformation felt different—stronger, more fluid. She landed on four paws and glanced down, her breath catching at the sight of her shimmering white coat.

"Ryker," she said through their mind-link, her voice filled with awe.

Ryker's massive black wolf stepped forward; his presence even more commanding than before. His coat seemed darker, almost absorbing the light around him, and his size was staggering.

"You're incredible," Ryker said, his voice reverent as he nudged her affectionately with his muzzle.

"Look at you," Lara replied, her wolf's voice filled with admiration.
They ran together through the forest, their movements perfectly in sync. The power coursing through them was undeniable, their bond stronger than ever.
When they finally slowed to a stop, Ryker turned to face her, his massive frame towering over hers.

"This is just the beginning, love," he said, his grey eyes gleaming. *"We're only getting started."*

Lara growled softly in agreement; her wolf filled with pride and contentment.

Together, they were unstoppable.

Chapter 13: New Challenges, New Beginnings

Lara sat at the large oak dining table in the mansion's meeting hall, watching as the senior members of the pack gathered around Ryker. The room hummed with tension. A vampire had been spotted near the northern border, a rarity that had everyone on edge.

Ryker stood at the head of the table, his commanding presence filling the room. His grey eyes swept over the gathered wolves, each one looking to him for guidance.

"The sighting has been confirmed," he said, his deep voice steady. "We don't know why it was here, but I won't take any chances. Vampires don't wander without purpose."

Lara's wolf growled softly in agreement, her instincts sharpening at the mention of the rogue predator.

One of the older pack members, a broad-shouldered wolf named Garrett, leaned forward. "Could it be a scout? Testing our defences?"

"It's possible," Ryker replied. "Which is why I'm doubling patrols along the northern border. I want reports every two hours."

"What if they're planning something bigger?" another wolf asked, his tone nervous.

Ryker's gaze hardened, his dominance rippling through the room. "Then we'll deal with it. This is our territory, and we will protect it."

Lara watched him with pride, admiring the way he commanded respect without needing to raise his voice. But she also sensed the

weight of the responsibility on his shoulders, the subtle tension in his jaw that only she would notice.
After the meeting ended, Ryker caught her by the arm as the others dispersed. "Are you okay?" he asked, his voice softening.

"I should be asking you that," Lara replied, stepping closer.

Ryker smiled faintly, his hands settling on her waist. "I'm fine. Just trying to make sure the pack knows we're ready for anything."

"And we are," Lara said, her voice steady.

Ryker nodded, his expression softening as he leaned down to kiss her. "I don't know what I'd do without you, love."
"You'll never have to find out," Lara promised, her wolf humming with satisfaction.

Stepping into Leadership

As Ryker managed the pack's defences, Lara found herself stepping into her role as alpha in new ways. She spent her mornings meeting with pack members, listening to their concerns and learning their stories.

One afternoon, she found herself sitting in the garden with a young wolf named Callie, who had just shifted for the first time.

"It was scary," Callie admitted, her voice trembling. "I didn't think I'd ever get it right."

"You're not alone," Lara said, placing a reassuring hand on the girl's shoulder. "Everyone feels that way at first. But you're stronger than you think, and you have a pack that will help you every step of the way."

Callie smiled hesitantly. "Thank you, Alpha Lara."

The title still felt strange, but it filled Lara with a sense of purpose. She wasn't just Ryker's mate—she was a leader, and the pack was beginning to see her as one.

A Visit Home

A few days later, Lara decided to visit her family. She hadn't seen them since the wedding, and the thought of spending time with her parents brought a wave of comfort.

Ryker insisted on driving her. As much as Lara had settled into her role, Ryker's protective instincts hadn't eased.

They arrived just before sunset, her mother rushing out to greet her with open arms.

"Lara!" she exclaimed, pulling her into a tight hug. "We've missed you."

"I've missed you too, Mum," Lara said, her heart swelling at the familiar warmth of home.

Her father stepped onto the porch, a smile softening his normally serious expression. "Welcome back, kiddo."

Lara smiled, hugging him tightly. "It's good to be home."

Inside, they shared stories over dinner, her mother fussing over her while her father asked about the pack. Ryker, ever the quiet observer, answered their questions with calm confidence.

Later, as they sat on the porch, her father turned to her, his voice low. "You're doing well, Lara. I can see it in your eyes. You're where you're meant to be."

Lara's chest swelled with emotion, and she nodded. "Thanks, Dad. That means a lot."

The Night Returns to Them

Back at the mansion, Lara leaned against the balcony railing, watching the stars. The cool night air brushed against her skin, but the warmth of Ryker's presence behind her was undeniable.

"You've been quiet," he murmured, his hands sliding around her waist.

"Just thinking," Lara replied, leaning into him.

"About what?"

"Everything," she admitted. "The pack, my family… you."

Ryker chuckled softly, his lips brushing against her ear. "I'm flattered."

Lara turned to face him; her gaze steady. "I don't know how you do it. Balancing everything—leading the pack, dealing with threats, keeping me sane."
"It's simple," Ryker said, his grey eyes darkening as he leaned closer. "I do it for you."

Her breath hitched as his hands tightened on her waist, pulling her flush against him. "Ryker…"
"I don't think you realize what you do to me," he growled, his voice rough with desire.
Lara's knees weakened as his lips claimed hers, the kiss deep and consuming. His dominance was unmistakable, his touch leaving her trembling as he guided her back inside.

The Change

The next morning, as they sat together in the kitchen, Ryker stilled suddenly, his sharp gaze locking onto her.

“Lara,” he said, his voice low and serious.

“What?” she asked, her heart skipping a beat at the intensity in his expression.

Ryker leaned closer, inhaling deeply. His grey eyes widened, and a slow, disbelieving smile spread across his face.

“Your scent,” he said softly, his voice filled with awe. “It’s changed.”

“What do you mean?” Lara asked, her wolf stirring uneasily.

Ryker reached for her hand; his grip gentle but firm. “You’re with child, Lara. You’re pregnant.”

Lara’s breath caught, her heart pounding as the words sank in. “Are you sure?”

Ryker nodded, his eyes glinting with both pride and love. “I’m sure. I can feel it. The bond is stronger now—it’s not just us anymore.”

Tears filled Lara’s eyes, and she placed a hand over her stomach, her wolf growling softly with approval. “We’re going to be parents.”

Ryker pulled her into his arms, his embrace fierce but tender. “You’ve just made me the happiest man in the world,” he murmured, his lips brushing against her hair.

As they held each other, the weight of the future felt lighter, their love a force that could overcome anything.

But in the back of Lara’s mind, a single thought lingered—the vampire.

Their bond had grown stronger, and with it, so had their family. But was this new life a blessing that would draw enemies even closer?

Chapter 14: Secrets and Surprises

The days following Ryker's revelation about Lara's pregnancy were some of the happiest she had ever experienced. The weight of their responsibilities felt lighter, softened by the secret they now shared.

Every time Ryker looked at her, she felt as though his gaze lingered just a moment longer, filled with a mixture of awe, pride, and fierce protectiveness. His dominant nature, which had always been a comforting constant, seemed to grow stronger with every passing day.

"You're mine," he told her one morning as they sat together in the mansion's sunlit garden, his hand resting possessively over her lower stomach.

"And I always will be," Lara replied, her fingers lacing with his.

Ryker smirked, leaning closer until their noses nearly touched. "You say that now, but you'll be begging for space soon enough, once I've got you wrapped in ten layers of protection."

Lara laughed, her wolf growling in playful protest. "I'm not fragile, Ryker."

"No," Ryker said, his voice dropping to a low, reverent tone. "You're not. But that doesn't mean I'm taking any chances."

Deciding to Keep the Secret

That same afternoon, as they walked through the halls of the mansion, Ryker stopped suddenly and turned to face her, his grey eyes dark with thought.

“We’re keeping this quiet,” he said firmly.

Lara tilted her head. “For how long?”

“For as long as we can,” Ryker replied. “At least until you’re further along. The pack doesn’t need distractions right now, not with the vampire threat hanging over us.”

She nodded, though a flicker of concern crossed her face. “But what if they notice? You said my scent’s already changing. And let’s be honest—Kate and Lilly are going to figure it out the moment they see me.”

Ryker’s lips twitched into a faint smile. “Let them guess. The rest of the pack will pick up on your glow eventually, but we’ll handle that when the time comes.”

His hand cupped her face, his thumb brushing gently over her cheek. “Right now, I just want to focus on you. On us.”

Lara leaned into his touch, her heart swelling with love. “Okay. We’ll keep it quiet. For now.”

Ryker's Protectiveness

The changes in Ryker's behaviour were subtle but impossible to miss. He shadowed her everywhere, always within arm's reach, his senses sharp and his movements deliberate.

"Ryker," Lara said one morning as she tried to head into the woods for a walk, only to find him blocking her path. "You're smothering me."

"I'm protecting you," Ryker corrected, his arms crossed. "There's a difference."
"I don't need protection from a walk," Lara argued, her wolf growling softly in agreement.

Ryker raised an eyebrow. "Maybe not. But until I'm sure there's no threat to our territory—or to you—you're not wandering off alone."

Lara huffed, though she couldn't deny the flicker of warmth in her chest at his devotion. "Fine. But you're walking with me."
Ryker's smirk returned. "I wouldn't have it any other way."

As they strolled through the woods, Ryker's hand settled on her lower back, his touch grounding. Lara's wolf purred in satisfaction, the bond between them stronger than ever.

A Visit to Her Parents

Later that week, Lara decided to visit her family. She hadn't been back home since the wedding, and the thought of her

mother's warm embrace and her father's steady presence brought a sense of comfort she didn't realize she needed.
Ryker insisted on driving her.
"You're not going alone," he said simply when she raised an eyebrow at his protective tone.
"I wasn't planning to," Lara replied with a smirk.

The drive was peaceful, the familiar countryside rolling past as they neared the small town of Kaiapoi. Ryker's hand rested on her knee, his thumb brushing slow circles against her skin.

When they arrived, her mother rushed out to greet them, pulling Lara into a tight hug.

"Lara, you look radiant," her mum said, stepping back to study her.

"She's been glowing lately," Ryker said, his tone warm but careful.

Lara shot him a subtle look, and he gave her a faint smirk in return.

Inside, the house felt as cozy as ever. The smell of freshly baked bread filled the air, and her father sat at the kitchen table, a smile softening his usually serious face.

"It's good to see you, kiddo," he said, standing to pull her into a brief hug.

"It's good to be back," Lara replied, her chest tightening with emotion.

As the evening wore on, they shared stories, laughter, and the warmth of family. Lara felt a pang of longing for these quiet moments, knowing that her new life at the mansion often felt worlds away from the simplicity of her childhood home.
Before they left, her father pulled her aside.

"You're doing well, Lara," he said, his voice low but filled with pride. "I can see it. You're where you're meant to be."

Lara nodded, tears prickling at the corners of her eyes. "Thanks, Dad."

The Glow

By the time they returned to the mansion, Ryker couldn't keep his hands off her.
"You were incredible today," he murmured as he pulled her into his arms, his grey eyes smouldering.

"Ryker," Lara began, laughing softly as his lips found her neck.

"You're glowing," he growled, his hands sliding over her waist. "And it's driving me insane."

Her breath hitched as he lifted her effortlessly, carrying her upstairs to their room. The door closed behind them with a soft click, and Lara surrendered to his touch, her wolf howling with approval.

Jessie's Arrival

The next evening, as the sun dipped below the horizon, the sound of a truck rumbling up the driveway caught Lara's attention.

She stood on the porch, her heart leaping as Jessie stepped out of the familiar vehicle.
"Jessie!" she called, rushing down the steps to meet him.
Jessie grinned, pulling her into a hug. "Lara, it's good to see you."
"It's been too long," Lara replied, stepping back to study him.

"I wasn't going to come empty-handed," Jessie said with a smirk, gesturing toward the truck.

The doors opened, and two men stepped out. Lara froze as recognition washed over her.

The first was tall and broad, his sandy blonde hair and sharp blue eyes unmistakable. The second was slightly shorter, his dark hair and rugged features giving him a more serious edge.

"Lara," Jessie said, his tone softening. "You remember my brothers, Caleb and Ben."

Lara's wolf stirred, a flood of memories from their childhood rushing back. Caleb and Ben had been her best friends once, their playful banter and adventurous spirits filling her early years with laughter. But they'd left for the army when she was still a teenager, and she hadn't seen them since.

"Caleb," Lara said, her voice barely above a whisper. "Ben."

"It's been a while," Caleb said, his smile warm but cautious.

"Too long," Ben added, his tone quieter but just as sincere.

Before Lara could respond, Jessie's expression turned serious.

"We need to talk," he said, his gaze flicking to Ryker, who had just joined them on the porch. "There's something you both need to know."

The weight of his words settled over them, and Lara felt the first stirrings of unease. Whatever news Jessie had brought, it was clear that their lives were about to change again.

Chapter 15: Bloodlines and Secrets

The air around the mansion felt charged as Jessie and his brothers stepped inside. Lara glanced between Caleb and Ben, her wolf stirring with recognition and unease. These weren't the carefree boys she remembered—they had grown into hardened men, their time in the military etched into their strong postures and watchful eyes.

Ryker's presence at her side was steady and grounding, but she couldn't ignore the curiosity crackling in the air as they all settled into the mansion's sitting room.

Jessie's face was grim as he leaned forward in his chair, his elbows resting on his knees. "What I'm about to tell you doesn't leave this room."

Lara exchanged a glance with Ryker, who gave her a small nod before addressing Jessie. "You have our trust. Speak."

Jessie let out a slow breath. "There's been movement in the north. A vampire clan has resurfaced, and we believe they've set their sights on your territory."

Lara's wolf bristled at the mention of vampires, her instincts sharpening. "Why here?"

Ben, who had been quiet until now, spoke up, his voice low and even. "Because of you."

Lara blinked, her gaze snapping to him. "Me?"

Caleb nodded; his blue eyes serious. "Vampires are drawn to power, Lara. And you and Ryker… you're not ordinary alphas. Your bond, your bloodlines—they make you a target."

Lara's hand instinctively went to her stomach, though she stopped herself before anyone could notice. "What do they want?"

"Control," Ben replied simply. "If they can't control you, they'll destroy you."
The words hung in the air like a dark cloud, but Ryker's voice cut through the tension with calm authority. "They won't get the chance."

Jessie nodded, though his expression remained grim. "We thought you'd say that. Which is why we're here. Caleb, Ben, and I—we want to help."

Lara's eyes widened. "You're offering to stay?"

"For as long as it takes," Caleb said, his voice firm.

Ryker studied them for a long moment before nodding. "We'll take all the help we can get. But know this: my pack, my mate, my rules."

"Understood," Ben said, his gaze steady.

Jessie smiled faintly. "Then I guess we're in this together."

The Visit to the Pack Doctor

The next morning, Lara sat in the pack doctor's office, the sterile scent of antiseptic filling her nose. Ryker sat beside her, his hand resting protectively on her thigh.

Dr. Elden, a kind-faced older wolf with silver hair, smiled reassuringly as he reviewed the results of Lara's initial checkup. "Well, there's no doubt about it. You're carrying a strong, healthy pup."

Lara felt a wave of relief wash over her, though Ryker's grip on her thigh tightened slightly. "Is there anything we need to be concerned about?" Ryker asked, his tone serious.
Dr. Elden hesitated for a moment before meeting their eyes. "There's something unique about pregnancies involving alphas, especially when both parents are… exceptional, as you two clearly are."

"Unique how?" Lara asked, her heart beginning to race.

"The baby will grow much faster than a typical wolf pregnancy," Dr. Elden explained. "Your body is strong enough to handle it, but you'll notice changes almost immediately. By the end of the second month, you'll appear close to full term."

Lara's breath caught. "That fast?"

Dr. Elden nodded. "It's not uncommon for alpha offspring. Your bond and your strength are accelerating the process. The good news is the baby is thriving. But you'll need to rest more than usual and avoid unnecessary stress."

Ryker's jaw tightened. "She'll be well taken care of. You have my word."

Lara placed her hand over Ryker's, giving him a reassuring squeeze. "We'll be fine, Ryker. I'm strong, remember?"

His gaze softened, though the protective fire in his eyes didn't fade. "You're strong," he agreed. "But I'm not taking any risks."

Strengthening Bonds

Back at the mansion, Lara sat in the garden with Caleb and Ben, catching up on lost years. They shared stories of their time in the army, their missions, and the bonds they'd formed with each other.

"You haven't changed much," Caleb said with a grin.

Lara raised an eyebrow. "I think I've changed quite a bit."

"Maybe," Caleb conceded. "But you're still the same Lara underneath it all. Fierce, stubborn, and too smart for your own good."

Ben chuckled softly, though his expression remained more serious. "He's not wrong. You always were the one keeping us out of trouble."

Lara laughed, her heart-warming at the familiarity of their banter. "And here I thought it was the other way around."

Intimate Moments

Later that night, Ryker found Lara in their room, staring out the window at the moonlit forest.

"You are quiet tonight," he said, his voice low as he approached her.

"Just thinking," Lara replied, leaning back into his chest as his arms wrapped around her.

"About the baby?"

"About everything," she admitted. "The baby, the pack, the vampires… it's a lot."

Ryker's lips brushed against her neck, his voice a soft growl. "You don't have to carry it all alone, love. That's why I'm here."
Lara turned to face him, her hands resting on his chest. "I know. And I love you for it."
Ryker's gaze darkened, his hands tightening on her waist. "You're mine, Lara. And I'll do whatever it takes to keep you safe."

Her breath hitched as his lips claimed hers, the kiss deep and consuming. His touch was firm, his dominance unmistakable as he lifted her effortlessly, carrying her to their bed.

The night stretched on, filled with whispered promises and the quiet hum of their bond. Lara surrendered completely, her wolf howling with satisfaction as Ryker's love and devotion surrounded her. He let his fingertips drift from the hollow of her throat down to the small of her back, each light trace sending a fresh wave of heat through her core. Her hands roamed his chest, feeling the sharp dip of each muscle, as he captured her mouth in a deep, claiming kiss. He brushed the sensitive seam of her thighs, barely there, and she trembled, legs parting instinctively.

She drew him closer, the slick slide of her body against his palm guiding him in a wordless invitation. When his mouth found hers again, it was all-consuming—hunger and worship intertwined in a kiss that left her dizzy with want.

The following morning, Lara joined Ryker, Jessie, Caleb, and Ben in the mansion's meeting room. Maps of their territory were spread across the table, marked with notes about patrols and possible vampire sightings.

"We need to tighten security along the eastern border," Ryker said, his voice steady. "That's where they're most likely to strike."

Caleb nodded; his expression thoughtful. "We'll take the lead on that patrol."

Before anyone could respond, one of the pack scouts burst into the room, his face pale.
"Alpha," he said, his voice trembling. "We've found something."

Ryker's expression darkened. "What is it?"

The scout hesitated, his gaze flicking to Lara. "A body. Near the northern border. Drained."

The room fell silent, the weight of the news settling over them like a storm cloud.

Ryker's hand found Lara's, his grip firm and reassuring. "We'll handle this," he said, his voice calm but filled with resolve.

But in Lara's heart, a new fear took root. The vampires weren't just watching—they were already here.

Chapter 16: Shadows in the Forest

The atmosphere in the mansion was heavy in the days following the discovery of the first body. Ryker and Jessie spent hours reviewing patrol reports and strengthening the pack's defences, while Caleb and Ben led small groups to scout the surrounding areas. Lara watched from the sidelines, torn between her desire to help and the growing realization that her condition limited her abilities.

She sat at the kitchen table, absentmindedly tracing patterns on the surface as her mind raced. Her wolf was restless, pacing inside her, frustrated by the lack of action.
"Lara," Ryker said softly, breaking her thoughts. He entered the room, his expression both gentle and commanding. "How are you feeling?"

Lara forced a smile. "I'm fine."

Ryker's gaze lingered on her, clearly unconvinced. He crossed the room and crouched in front of her, his hands resting on her knees. "You're not fine. Talk to me."
She sighed, her shoulders slumping. "I just feel… useless. Everyone is out there protecting the pack, and I'm stuck here."

Ryker's hand moved to her stomach, his touch steady and grounding. "You're protecting our future, Lara. That's more important than anything else."

Her chest tightened at the sincerity in his voice, but it didn't ease the frustration swirling inside her.

The Investigation Deepens

Later that day, Jessie and Ben returned to the mansion, their expressions grim. Ryker called a meeting in the main hall, where Lara joined him despite her growing exhaustion.
"We found another body," Jessie announced, his tone clipped. "This time, it's worse."

Ryker's jaw tightened. "What do you mean?"

"It was a student from the high school," Ben said, his voice heavy. "The body was left near the western edge of the territory. Drained completely, just like the first."

Lara's breath caught, her mind reeling. She thought of the students she'd graduated with, their faces flashing through her memory.

"It's on the news," Jessie added. "The humans think it's some kind of wild animal attack, but the details are spreading fast."

Ryker's gaze darkened; his wolf barely contained. "They're sending a message."

Lara's stomach churned, and she gripped the back of a chair for support. "If they're trying to scare us, it's working." To think one of her friends has lost their lives because of her and Ryker.

"We can't let them win," Ryker said firmly, his hand brushing against hers. "We'll increase patrols and keep a closer watch on the borders. I'm bringing more of our strongest wolves back to the pack." Jessie nodded. "We'll need everyone we can get."

Lara's Struggles

As the meeting dispersed, Lara lingered in the hall, her mind racing. The guilt weighed heavily on her. The thought crept into her mind like a shadow—*If I left, would it save them?* Her wolf growled softly in protest, but the idea was difficult to shake. If the vampires were targeting the pack because of her and Ryker's bond, maybe her absence could change everything. But as she glanced toward Ryker, who stood with Jessie discussing patrols, her chest tightened. She couldn't imagine leaving him, not now—not ever.

A Visit to the Doctor

A few days later, Lara sat in the pack doctor's office again, her anxiety bubbling under the surface. Ryker sat beside her, his hand resting on her knee as they waited for Dr. Elden to enter.

When the doctor arrived, he greeted them with a warm smile. "How are we feeling today?"

"Restless," Lara admitted. "I need to ask you something."

Dr. Elden raised an eyebrow, gesturing for her to continue. "Is it safe for me to shift?" Lara asked, her voice trembling slightly.

Dr. Elden's expression turned serious. "Lara, with the rate your pup is growing, shifting is extremely risky. The strain it would put on your body—and the baby—could be catastrophic."

Lara's chest tightened, and she glanced at Ryker, whose jaw had clenched at the doctor's words.
"She won't be shifting," Ryker said firmly, his tone leaving no room for argument.

Lara bristled, her frustration bubbling to the surface. "I'm not fragile, Ryker."

"No," he said, turning to face her, his grey eyes blazing. "You're not. But you're carrying our pup, Lara. And I'm not risking either of you."
Dr. Elden cleared his throat gently. "With proper care, you'll be fine, Lara. Focus on rest and let your body do what it needs to."
The doctor's reassurances did little to soothe her. As they left the office, Lara felt the weight of her limitations pressing down on her, her wolf growling in quiet frustration.

Finding Purpose

Back at the mansion, Lara sought out the pack's women, many of whom had gathered in the kitchen to prepare food for the patrol teams.

"Mind if I join?" Lara asked, her tone hesitant.

The women exchanged glances before one of them, a motherly wolf named Maeve, smiled warmly. "Of course, Alpha. We'd love the help."

As Lara rolled up her sleeves and joined the group, she found herself immersed in their stories. Maeve spoke of raising three

rambunctious boys, while another woman, Tessa, shared tales of her own adventures before joining the pack.
For the first time in days, Lara felt a sense of belonging. The kitchen buzzed with laughter and warmth, and her frustration began to ease as she focused on chopping vegetables and kneading dough.

Plans for Defence

Meanwhile, Ryker, Jessie, Caleb, and Ben worked tirelessly to organize the pack's defences. Stronger wolves were called back to the territory, their arrival bringing a sense of renewed determination.

Patrols were doubled, and plans were drawn up for how to respond to a vampire attack. The pack buzzed with activity, their loyalty to Ryker and Lara unwavering.

"Everyone knows their role," Jessie said as he and Ryker stood on the mansion's balcony, overlooking the training grounds below.

Ryker nodded. "Good. Because this isn't just about protecting the pack. It's about sending a message—they won't win."

A Shocking Discovery

That evening, as the patrols returned, a commotion erupted near the mansion's entrance. Lara rushed outside, Ryker close behind, to find a group of wolves standing in a protective circle around a figure.

“What’s going on?” Ryker demanded, his voice sharp.
One of the patrol members stepped forward, his expression grim. “We found her near the northern border. She’s… young.”

Lara’s breath caught as she stepped closer, her wolf growling softly. The figure at the centre of the group was a girl, no older than fourteen, her pale skin and glowing red eyes unmistakable.

“A vampire,” Ryker growled, his body tensing beside Lara.

The girl looked up, her expression a mix of fear and defiance. “I didn’t mean to cross,” she said, her voice trembling. “Please… don’t hurt me.”
Lara’s wolf stilled, her instincts warring with her curiosity. Who was this girl? And why had she come here?

Ryker’s grey eyes locked onto the girl; his expression unreadable. “We’ll see.”

Chapter 17: Joy, Secrets, and Support

The mansion hummed with quiet activity as Lara stood in front of the full-length mirror in her bedroom, her hands gently resting on her stomach. The changes were subtle but undeniable now—her lower abdomen had begun to curve, her pregnancy finally starting to show.

A soft knock sounded at the door.

"Come in," Lara called.

Ryker entered; his grey eyes immediately drawn to her reflection. His lips curved into a slow smile as he crossed the room, his hands settling on her hips from behind.

"You're glowing," he murmured, his voice filled with awe.

"Am I?" Lara teased, leaning back against him.

"Always," he replied, brushing a kiss against her neck.

Her wolf purred in contentment as Ryker's hands moved to her stomach, his touch warm and protective. "Have you felt him yet?" he asked softly.

"Not yet," Lara said, though her heart raced at the thought.

"Soon," Ryker promised, his voice thick with emotion. "He's strong. Just like his mother."

Interrogating the Girl

The following morning, Lara joined Ryker and the senior pack members in the study, where the young vampire sat in a chair under the watchful eyes of Jessie, Caleb, and Ben. Her pale skin and red eyes stood out starkly in the warm wood-panelled room, but her small frame and trembling hands reminded Lara just how young she was.

Ryker leaned forward; his grey eyes sharp. "What's your name?"

"Emilia," the girl said, her voice barely above a whisper.

"Why were you on our territory?" Ryker asked, his tone calm but commanding.

"I ran away," Emilia said, her gaze darting nervously around the room. "I didn't want to be part of their plans."

"Whose plans?" Jessie pressed.

"The elders," Emilia replied, her voice trembling. "They're planning something big—something against your pack. They say your alphas are a threat, that you'll destroy everything they've worked for."

Lara's stomach churned, her hand instinctively moving to her growing belly.

"What else do you know?" Ryker asked, his voice cold.

“They’re sending scouts,” Emilia said. “But they don’t know I’m here. If they find out…” Her voice faltered, tears welling in her eyes. “Please, I don’t want to go back. Don’t send me back.”

Lara’s wolf growled softly in her mind, torn between sympathy and suspicion.

“We’ll decide what to do with you,” Ryker said, his tone firm. “For now, you’re staying here. Under guard.”

Sharing the News

Later that day, Ryker called the pack together in the main hall. Lara’s parents had been invited, along with Kate, Lilly, and a few close friends. The room buzzed with curiosity and anticipation as everyone gathered.

Ryker stood beside Lara; his arm wrapped protectively around her waist. When the room quieted, he cleared his throat.

“Lara and I have something to share,” he began, his voice steady but warm. “We’re expecting a child.”

A ripple of gasps and murmurs swept through the crowd, followed quickly by cheers and applause. Lara’s mother burst into tears, pulling her daughter into a tight hug while her father beamed with pride.

Kate and Lilly squealed in excitement, rushing to embrace Lara.

“A baby?” Kate said, her voice filled with awe. “That’s amazing!”

“When did you find out?” Lilly asked, her grin wide.

“A little while ago,” Lara admitted, her cheeks flushing.

Her parents hugged Ryker tightly, her mother dabbing at her eyes. “A grandchild,” she said, her voice trembling with joy. “Oh, Lara, we’re so happy for you.”
Ryker smiled warmly. “He’s going to have the best family.”

“He?” Lara’s father asked, raising an eyebrow.

Lara laughed, nodding. “We found out yesterday. It’s a boy.”

The room erupted into more cheers; the excitement contagious. For the first time in weeks, Lara felt a true sense of joy and belonging.

Bonding with the Pack and Friends

Over the next few days, Lara found herself spending more time with the pack’s women. Maeve and Tessa had taken her under their wing, introducing her to the other mothers-to-be. They baked together in the mornings, filling the kitchen with the scent of fresh bread and cookies, and spent afternoons reading to the pack’s children in the library.

“It’s important to keep busy,” Maeve said one day as they worked side by side in the kitchen. “Especially with everything going on. It keeps the mind from wandering too much.”

Lara smiled faintly, her thoughts drifting to the vampires and Emilia's warnings. "I think you're right," she said softly.

Her friends, Kate and Lilly, had decided to stay for a while, sensing that Lara needed their presence. They spent evenings reminiscing about their school days, laughing over old memories and teasing Lara about her pregnancy glow.

"She's practically radiant," Kate said one night as they sat in Lara's room, drinking tea.

"It's almost unfair," Lilly added with a grin. "How do you look this good while pregnant?"

Lara laughed; her heart full. "Trust me, I don't always feel this good."

Confiding in Jessie

One afternoon, Lara found Jessie standing watch near the forest's edge. She approached him quietly, her wolf stirring at the sight of one of her most trusted friends.

"Hey," she said softly.

Jessie turned, his expression softening. "Hey, Lara. What's on your mind?"

She hesitated before speaking, her voice low. "I've been feeling… stuck. Like I need to get out, stretch my paws, do something normal. This is supposed to be the best time of my life, but I feel like I'm trapped."

Jessie frowned, his gaze searching hers. "You're not trapped, Lara. But I get it. You need some space."

She nodded, her chest tightening. "I was thinking about taking some of the ladies' baby shopping. It might help, you know? But convincing Ryker…"

Jessie smirked. "Leave that to me. I'll talk to him—and I'll make sure your friends keep you busy until then."

Lara smiled gratefully. "Thanks, Jessie. I don't know what I'd do without you."

Planning Ahead

That evening, Jessie pulled Kate and Lilly aside, his tone serious.

"Lara's feeling restless," he said. "She needs you to keep her grounded right now. Keep her busy, distract her—whatever it takes."

Kate nodded. "We'll do whatever she needs."

"She's not alone in this," Lilly added. "We'll stay as long as it takes."

The First Movements

That night, as Lara lay in bed, she felt it—a faint fluttering sensation in her abdomen, like the soft brush of butterfly wings.

"Ryker," she whispered, nudging him awake.

“What is it?” he asked, instantly alert.

“I felt him,” Lara said, her voice trembling with emotion.

Ryker’s face softened, and he placed his hand over her stomach. Moments later, the flutter came again, stronger this time.

“He’s moving,” Ryker murmured, his voice filled with awe. “That’s our son.”
Tears filled Lara’s eyes, and she smiled. “Our son.”
The next morning, as the pack gathered to discuss patrol plans, one of the scouts burst into the room, his face pale.

“Alpha,” he said, his voice shaking. “We’ve found something.”

“What is it?” Ryker demanded.

“A trail,” the scout replied. “Leading straight to us.”

The room fell silent, the weight of his words sinking in. Lara’s wolf growled softly, her instincts sharpening as she met Ryker’s gaze.

“They’re coming,” Ryker said, his voice low but resolute.

Chapter 18: The Awakening

The tension in the pack grew sharper with each passing day. The discovery of the vampire trail had sent a ripple of unease through the mansion, and Lara could feel the weight of it pressing on everyone's shoulders. Patrols were doubled, strong wolves called back from distant posts, and Ryker's command became a steadying force for the pack.

For Lara, the unease was more personal. It wasn't just the vampires or the mounting responsibilities as an alpha. It was the dreams.

They had started quietly, creeping into her nights like whispers from a forgotten past. At first, they were fragmented images of the forest bathed in silver moonlight, flashes of her grandmother's familiar face, and the pulsing glow of the crescent moon necklace. But now, they were growing more vivid, almost tangible, and she could no longer ignore them.

The First Dream

Lara woke with a start, her breath coming in short gasps. The dream had been so real. She had been standing in the middle of a dense forest, her white wolf glowing faintly in the moonlight. Her grandmother had been there too, younger and more vibrant than Lara remembered, her dark hair streaked with grey, her eyes sharp and full of purpose.

Her grandmother's lips had moved, forming words, but no sound came out. She had gestured to the necklace, which glowed against her chest in sync with the light emanating from Lara's wolf. Her expression was urgent, her eyes pleading, but as Lara stepped closer, the image shattered like glass.

She sat up in bed, clutching the necklace instinctively. It was warm to the touch, as though it had absorbed the remnants of the dream.

"What is happening to me?" she whispered into the dark.

Ryker's Scepticism

The next morning, Lara sat at the breakfast table, poking at her food as Ryker and Jessie discussed patrol strategies.

"You're quiet this morning," Ryker said, his grey eyes studying her carefully.
Lara hesitated before speaking. "I've been having dreams," she admitted, her voice low.

Ryker raised an eyebrow. "Dreams?"

"They're about my grandmother," Lara explained. "She's trying to tell me something about the necklace. But I can't hear her. It's like… she's reaching out from somewhere I can't quite touch."

Jessie glanced at the necklace; his expression thoughtful. "That thing has always been a little strange, hasn't it?"

Lara nodded, turning the crescent moon pendant over in her hand. "It's always been special, but now it feels… alive. Like it's connected to me in some way."

Ryker frowned; his scepticism evident. "Dreams are just dreams, Lara. You've been under a lot of stress lately—it's probably your mind trying to process everything."

"But what if it's more than that?" Lara asked, her frustration bubbling to the surface.

"There are old legends about the white

wolf, about an alpha who could unite the unlikeliest of allies." Ryker leaned back in his chair, crossing his arms. "Legends, Lara. Stories passed down to entertain pups. I wouldn't put too much stock in them."

Lara's wolf bristled at his dismissive tone, but she took a steadying breath. "I can't ignore this, Ryker. Something is happening to me, and I need to figure out what it means."

Ryker's gaze softened, and he reached out to take her hand. "If it's important to you, we'll figure it out. Together."

The Prophecy

Lara decided to seek out Maeve, who had spent years gathering the oral histories and legends of their pack. The older wolf was sitting in the library, surrounded by dusty books and scrolls, when Lara entered.

"Alpha," Maeve said warmly, motioning for Lara to sit. "What brings you here?"

Lara hesitated before speaking. "I need to know about the legends. The ones about the white wolf."

Maeve's expression turned serious as she leaned forward. "Ah, the old stories. They've been passed down for generations. What do you want to know?"

Lara ran her fingers over the crescent moon pendant. "Is there anything about a necklace? Or about an alpha who could unite wolves and vampires?"

Maeve's eyes widened slightly. "There is. But those stories are ancient, even older than most of the pack remembers.
They speak of an alpha born into a powerful bloodline, marked by a white wolf and a connection to the crescent moon."

“What does it mean?” Lara asked, her voice trembling slightly.

Maeve’s gaze softened. “The prophecy says that this alpha would have the power to bridge the divide between wolves and vampires, to end the centuries of bloodshed. But it comes at a great cost. The power can only be invoked by the strongest alpha—one who carries not just strength, but compassion, wisdom, and courage.”

Lara’s heart raced as Maeve continued. “The necklace is said to hold that power, but it cannot be activated until the chosen alpha proves themselves worthy. Once invoked, the power becomes part of them forever.”

“Has anyone ever invoked it before?” Lara asked.

Maeve shook her head. “If they have, the stories don’t tell us. But if the legends are true, that alpha is you, Lara.”

A Growing Realization

Lara left the library in a daze, her mind racing with questions. Could she really be the alpha from the prophecy? The thought was overwhelming, yet it resonated deep within her.

She wandered through the mansion’s halls until she found Ryker in the training yard, overseeing a group of wolves practicing their shifts.

“You’re thinking too much again,” Ryker said, his smirk softening as he approached her.
Lara shook her head, her voice steady despite the whirlwind of emotions inside her. “Maeve confirmed the legends.
She thinks the prophecy is about me.”

Ryker frowned, his grey eyes narrowing. “Lara…”

"I know what you're going to say," she interrupted. "That it's just a story. But what if it's not? What if this is why the vampires are coming? What if this is my purpose?"

Ryker sighed, his hands settling on her shoulders. "I believe in you, Lara. But I'm not ready to believe in some ancient legend. Not yet."

Lara met his gaze, her determination unwavering. "I don't need you to believe in the legend, Ryker. I just need you to believe in me."

"I do," he said softly, pulling her into his arms. "Always."

The Necklace's Glow

That night, as Lara lay in bed, the crescent moon pendant pulsed faintly against her chest. The dreams returned, clearer this time. She saw her grandmother standing in the forest again, her lips moving silently as she gestured to the necklace.

The glow from the pendant spread, surrounding Lara in a warm, golden light. She felt a strange sense of peace, as though the necklace itself was reassuring her.

When she woke, she clutched the pendant tightly, her wolf growling softly with resolve. Whatever this power was, she would learn to understand it.

Chapter 19: The White Stag

The tension in the pack was palpable as preparations for the vampire threat continued. Patrols scouted the borders day and night, and strategies were laid out to protect the territory. Yet despite the constant activity, Lara felt the undercurrent of something larger brewing beneath the surface—a pull she couldn't ignore.

Her dreams had grown more vivid, filled with flashes of her grandmother and the crescent moon necklace glowing brighter than ever. The forest always played a part in these visions, its silver-lit shadows calling to her like a whispered invitation.

She didn't know why, but she felt the answers she sought lay beyond the mansion's walls, waiting for her in the trees.

A Walk in the Woods

That morning, Lara stood at the edge of the forest, her hand resting protectively on her stomach. She could feel her wolf pacing inside her, eager for movement despite Dr. Elden's warnings about shifting.

"Are you sure about this?" Ryker's voice came from behind her, steady but tinged with concern.

"I need some air," Lara replied, turning to meet his gaze. "And I need to think."

Ryker hesitated before nodding. "I'll come with you."

Lara gave him a faint smile. "You don't always have to protect me, you know."

"Yes, I do," Ryker said simply, falling into step beside her.

They walked in silence, the cool breeze carrying the scent of pine and damp earth. The forest felt alive, its energy thrumming through Lara's senses as though it were aware of her presence.

And then she saw it.

The White Stag

The stag stepped out from the shadows like a ghost, its coat as white as freshly fallen snow. Its antlers were enormous, spreading wide like the branches of an ancient tree, and its luminous eyes locked onto Lara's with an intelligence that sent a shiver down her spine.

Ryker froze beside her, his wolf growling softly. The rest of the pack, who had been trailing them at a respectful distance, stopped in their tracks, their murmurs of disbelief barely audible.

"A white stag," Ryker said under his breath. "That's… impossible."

The stag moved with slow, deliberate steps until it stood before Lara. Then, to the astonishment of everyone present, it lowered itself onto its knees, bowing its massive head in submission.

Lara's breath caught, her wolf stilling in awe. She was vaguely aware of the pack's gasps behind her, but the world seemed to fade until it was just her and the stag.

Compelled by something she couldn't explain, Lara stepped forward. She reached out a trembling hand, her fingers brushing against the stag's soft fur.

"You're magnificent," she whispered, her voice barely audible.

The stag lifted its head slightly, its luminous eyes meeting hers with an intensity that seemed to pierce her soul. For a moment, it felt as though the forest itself had stilled, holding its breath in reverence.

And then, as suddenly as it had appeared, the stag turned and disappeared into the trees, leaving silence in its wake.

The Realization

Lara turned back to the group, her cheeks flushed and her heart racing. The pack members stood in stunned silence, their expressions a mix of awe and disbelief.

Ryker's grey eyes were locked onto her, his usual stoicism replaced by something softer—something that looked suspiciously like acceptance.
"It bowed to you," he said, his voice low.

"It… did," Lara replied, her voice trembling.

Ryker took a step closer, his gaze searching hers. "Do you understand what this means?"

Lara nodded slowly. "The prophecy is real. And I'm the one it's about."

For the first time, Ryker didn't argue. He didn't dismiss the legends or offer a logical explanation. Instead, he reached out, his hands settling on her shoulders.

"I believe you," he said softly.

The weight of his words settled over her, both reassuring and terrifying.

Plans for the Vampires

That evening, Lara and Ryker gathered with Jessie, Caleb, Ben, and the senior pack members in the mansion's strategy room. A map of their territory was spread across the table, marked with potential points of attack.

"The stag's appearance changes things," Ryker began, his tone firm. "We're not just dealing with a vampire threat. We're dealing with a prophecy—and Lara's role in it."

"What does the prophecy mean for us?" Caleb asked, his brow furrowed.

"It means the vampires might be after more than just territory," Jessie said. "If they know about the prophecy—and they likely do—they could see Lara as a threat to their power."

Lara's wolf growled softly, and she placed a hand over her stomach. "If the prophecy is true, then I'm meant to stop this war. But I can't do that without understanding the necklace or its power."

"Then we'll protect you until you're ready," Ryker said, his grey eyes steady. "No one gets near you. Not the vampires, not anyone."

Jessie nodded. "We'll increase patrols around the mansion. No one comes in or out without us knowing."

"And what about Emilia?" Ben asked. "She's still locked in the cellar. She might know more than she's letting on.

"I'll speak with her," Ryker said.
"If there's anything she hasn't told us, we'll find out."

A Private Moment

Later that night, Lara sat on the balcony of their room, staring out at the moonlit forest. The memory of the stag was still fresh in her mind; its luminous eyes and gentle bow etched into her thoughts.

"You were incredible today," Ryker said, stepping outside to join her.

Lara glanced up at him, a faint smile tugging at her lips. "You believe it now, don't you? The prophecy?"

"I believe in you," Ryker said simply, sitting beside her.

They sat in comfortable silence for a moment before Lara spoke again. "Do you think I'll be ready when the time comes? To use the necklace, to end this war?"

Ryker reached for her hand, his grip firm but gentle. "You've always been ready, Lara. You just don't see it yet."

Her wolf growled softly in agreement, and for the first time in days, she felt a flicker of hope.

A Warning from Emilia

The next morning, Ryker and Lara descended into the cellar to speak with Emilia. The young vampire looked smaller than ever in the dim light, her red eyes wide and wary.

"They're coming," she said before Ryker could speak.
"What do you mean?" Ryker demanded, his tone sharp.

"They know about her," Emilia whispered, glancing nervously at Lara. "About the prophecy. They're coming for her."
The words sent a chill through Lara, her wolf bristling with both fear and determination.

“How soon?” Ryker asked, his voice deadly calm.
“Soon,” Emilia said, her voice trembling. “And they won’t stop until they have her.”

Chapter 20: Bloodlines and Allies

The days following Emilia's warning were a blur of activity. Patrols were doubled, and every able-bodied wolf in the pack was assigned a role, from border scouts to night guards. The mansion became a hub of preparation, with maps spread across tables, strategies debated late into the night, and weapons quietly distributed to those who might need them.

But for Lara, life had taken on a different rhythm.

Her pregnancy was progressing rapidly now, her belly rounding visibly in a way that would have been alarming if she weren't already expecting it. She was constantly hungry, and the sheer exhaustion she felt at times made her wolf bristle with frustration.

"Do you want more soup?" Ryker asked one evening, watching as she cradled a bowl on the couch.

"More?" Lara teased, though her stomach growled softly in response. "I've had three bowls already."

"And you're eating for two," Ryker replied, his tone firm but warm.

She rolled her eyes, though her smile betrayed her amusement. "I might have some bread."

Ryker smirked, already heading to the kitchen.

Lara leaned back with a sigh, her hand resting on her belly. The baby's movements were more frequent now—little flutters and kicks that filled her with a sense of wonder. Her wolf purred contentedly, even as exhaustion tugged at her mind.

Dreaming of Emilia

That night, Lara's dreams returned, sharper and more vivid than ever. She was in the forest again, but this time she wasn't alone.

A young girl stood before her—Emilia. Her pale skin and crimson eyes glowed softly in the moonlight, but her expression wasn't one of menace. Instead, it was filled with fear and sadness.
"They're coming," Emilia said, her voice trembling. "You have to stop them."

"How?" Lara asked, her voice carrying in the stillness.

"By saving me," Emilia replied, her gaze pleading.

Before Lara could respond, the dream shifted. The crescent moon necklace pulsed against her chest, its glow intensifying as her grandmother's face appeared briefly in the shadows. The words she couldn't hear before were now clear, ringing through the dream like a prophecy:

"Protect the innocent. Bridge the divide. The power is yours, but the choice is theirs."

When Lara woke, her heart was pounding. She sat up in bed, clutching the necklace as its warmth lingered against her skin.

"What is it?" Ryker asked, his voice heavy with sleep as he stirred beside her.

"Emilia," Lara said softly. "I need to talk to her.

The Truth About Emilia

Later that morning, Lara descended into the cellar where Emilia was being kept. The young vampire looked up as she entered, her red eyes wide with fear.

"Alpha," one of the guards said, stepping aside to let Lara approach.

"Leave us," Lara said, her tone gentle but firm.

The guards hesitated before nodding, exiting the room and leaving Lara and Emilia alone.

"I dreamed about you," Lara began, sitting down on a low stool across from the girl.

Emilia blinked; her expression wary. "You did?"

"Yes," Lara said. "And I think there's more to you than you've been telling us."

Emilia's shoulders tensed, and she looked away. "You wouldn't believe me if I told you."

"Try me," Lara said softly.

For a long moment, Emilia was silent. Then she sighed, her voice barely above a whisper. "I'm the leader's daughter."

Lara's breath caught, her wolf growling softly in surprise. "The leader of your coven?"

Emilia nodded. "My father. He's the one who sent the scouts. He's the one who wants you dead."

"Why did you leave?" Lara asked, her tone gentle.

Emilia's gaze flicked to her, and tears filled her crimson eyes. "Because I don't believe in what they're doing. I never have. My father… he used to want peace too. He said there was a time when wolves and vampires could live together. But when he found out about you and Ryker—your bond, your power—he became obsessed. He thinks you're a threat to everything we've built."

"And what do you think?" Lara asked.

"I think…" Emilia hesitated, her voice trembling. "I think you might be the only one who can stop him."

Lara's Decision

Lara sat back, her mind racing. Emilia's words echoed in her ears, and the memory of her grandmother's voice in the dream filled her with a strange sense of purpose.

"You're not my enemy, are you?" Lara asked.

"No," Emilia said, shaking her head. "I hate what my coven has become. I don't want this war. I just… I want peace."

Lara's wolf growled softly in agreement, and she reached out, placing a hand on Emilia's shoulder. "Then I'll protect you."

Emilia's eyes widened. "You would do that? Even knowing who I am?"

"Yes," Lara said firmly. "Because this isn't just about me. It's about all of us—wolves and vampires. If we don't stop this war, it will destroy everything."

Preparing for What's to Come

When Lara returned to the main hall, Ryker was waiting for her, his expression tense.

"What did she say?" he asked.

Lara hesitated before meeting his gaze. "She's the leader's daughter. And she wants peace."

Ryker's jaw tightened, and his grey eyes darkened. "That doesn't mean we can trust her."

"I believe her," Lara said, her voice steady.
Ryker stared at her for a long moment before sighing, his shoulders relaxing slightly. "If you trust her, I'll trust her. But we need to be ready for anything."

They spent the rest of the day finalizing preparations. Wolves were assigned to patrols and guard duty, and plans were drawn up for how to defend the mansion if an attack came.

Jessie, Caleb, and Ben took charge of training the younger wolves, while Maeve worked with Lara to review the ancient texts about the prophecy.

A Moment of Quiet

That evening, as the sun dipped below the horizon, Lara and Ryker stood on the balcony of their room, gazing out at the forest.

"Do you think we can stop this?" Lara asked softly, her hand resting on her belly.Ryker reached out, wrapping an arm around her waist. "I don't know," he admitted. "But I know we'll fight for it. For you. For him."

Lara smiled faintly, her heart swelling with love. “He’s getting stronger,” she said, feeling the baby kick gently beneath her hand.
Ryker’s hand joined hers, his eyes softening. “Just like his mother.”

They stood in silence for a while, the weight of their responsibilities hanging between them. But for that moment, Lara allowed herself to hope.

The next morning, the sound of hurried footsteps echoed through the mansion. A scout burst into the strategy room, his face pale.

“Alpha,” he said breathlessly. “They’re here.”

Ryker’s expression darkened as he rose to his feet. “How many?”

“Dozens,” the scout replied. “But they’re not attacking. They’re… waiting.”

“Waiting for what?” Lara asked, her wolf growling softly.

The scout’s gaze flicked to her, his voice trembling. “For you.”

Chapter 21: The Battle Begins

The tension in the mansion was suffocating. Wolves paced the halls, their growls rumbling softly as they waited for orders. Lara stood at the large window in the main hall, staring out at the forest. She could feel it in the air—a storm brewing just beyond the tree line, ready to crash down on them at any moment.

Ryker entered the room, his expression hard and commanding. He moved with a purpose, his grey eyes scanning every detail, every wolf, and every moment.

“Lara,” he said firmly, stopping in front of her.
She turned to meet his gaze, her wolf stirring restlessly. “I need to be there.” “No,” Ryker said, his voice low but unyielding. “You’re staying here.”

“Ryker—”

“You are not risking yourself or our son,” he growled, cutting her off. “This isn’t up for debate.”

Lara’s chest tightened, her frustration rising, but she knew better than to push him further. Ryker’s protectiveness had grown tenfold since her pregnancy became visible, and while she hated feeling sidelined, she also understood his fear.

“I’ll be safe,” Lara said softly, trying to ease the tension. “I can handle myself, Ryker.”

Ryker’s jaw clenched, and he placed his hands on her shoulders, leaning closer. “I know you can. But I won’t let you.” His voice softened slightly, but the steel in his gaze didn’t waver. “Stay here, Lara. Promise me.”
After a long pause, Lara nodded reluctantly. “I promise.”

Ryker straightened, his grey eyes flicking to Jessie, who stood near the door. "Guards will stay with her at all times. No one gets near the mansion without my permission."

Jessie nodded; his expression unreadable. "Consider it done."

The Perimeter Holds

Ryker's team assembled quickly at the edge of the forest, their formation tight and disciplined. Caleb and Ben stood to his right; their expressions grim but focused. Jessie joined them moments later, his eyes scanning the shadows ahead.

"They've moved closer," Jessie said, nodding toward the tree line. "We spotted movement about fifty yards in."

Ryker growled softly, his wolf bristling with anticipation. "How many?"

"Too many to count," Caleb replied. "But they're holding their ground for now."

"They're testing us," Ben added, his voice low.

Ryker nodded, his jaw tightening. "Then let's show them why that's a mistake."

The wolves shifted into position, their movements sharp and precise. The clearing fell silent, the air thick with tension as they waited for the inevitable.

The First Strike

The attack came without warning.
A blur of motion shot from the shadows, and the first vampire leaped into the clearing, its fangs bared and eyes glowing

crimson. Ryker shifted mid-movement, his massive black wolf charging forward to meet the attack head-on.
The vampire snarled, claws slashing through the air, but Ryker's wolf was faster. He lunged, his jaws closing around the vampire's arm with bone-crushing force.

The clearing erupted into chaos as more vampires poured from the trees, their movements swift and deadly. The wolves surged forward, their growls and snarls blending into a deafening roar as they collided with their enemies.

Lara's Restlessness

Back at the mansion, Lara paced the main hall, her wolf growling softly in frustration. The distant sounds of battle reached her ears, faint but unmistakable, and her instincts screamed at her to act.

"Lara," Jessie said, stepping into the room. "You need to stay here."

"I know," Lara said, her tone sharper than she intended. "But that doesn't make it any easier."

Jessie hesitated before nodding. "They'll handle it. Ryker knows what he's doing."

Lara sighed, her hand resting on her belly. "I just hate feeling useless."

"You're not useless," Jessie said firmly. "You're doing the most important thing anyone can do—protecting your family."

Lara managed a small smile, though the tension in her chest didn't ease.

The Battle Intensifies

In the clearing, the fight raged on. Ryker's wolf tore through another vampire, his massive form a blur of motion as he defended his pack.

Caleb and Ben fought side by side, their wolves working in perfect sync to overpower a group of three vampires. Nearby, Jessie's wolf darted between two attackers, his agility unmatched as he delivered a swift, lethal blow to one of them.

But for every vampire that fell, another seemed to take its place.

"They're not letting up!" Caleb growled, his voice echoing through the mind-link.

"Hold the line!" Ryker commanded, his voice firm.

The wolves rallied, their strength and unity driving them forward. But even as they pushed the vampires back, Ryker's instincts screamed that this was only the beginning.

An Uneasy Calm

Hours later, the vampires retreated into the forest, their numbers thinned but not defeated. Ryker shifted back; his breathing heavy as he surveyed the battlefield.

"They'll be back," Jessie said, shifting into his human form beside him. "This was just a test."

Ryker nodded; his expression grim. "We need to be ready."

Lara Learns the Truth

When Ryker returned to the mansion, Lara was waiting for him in the main hall. Her wolf stirred at the sight of him, relief flooding through her as she rushed to meet him.

“You’re okay,” she said, her voice trembling.

“I’m fine,” Ryker replied, pulling her into a tight embrace.

“What happened?” Lara asked, pulling back to look at him.

Ryker’s expression darkened. “It was a test. They wanted to see how strong we are.”

Lara’s chest tightened, and her hand instinctively moved to her necklace. “And?”
“They know we won’t go down without a fight,” Ryker said. “But this isn’t over.”

Darius’s Warning

That night, as the pack gathered to regroup, a scout arrived with a grim message.

“Alpha,” he said, his voice trembling. “We found this near the northern border.”

He handed Ryker a scrap of parchment, the edges burned. Ryker unfolded it carefully, his expression hardening as he read the words scrawled in blood-red ink:

This is just the beginning. She belongs to us.

The room fell silent, the weight of the message pressing down on everyone.
“They’re coming for her,” Ryker said, his voice a low growl.

Lara's wolf bristled, and her hand tightened around the crescent moon pendant. "Let them try."

Chapter 22: A Line Crossed

The battle was chaos. Wolves clashed with vampires, their growls and snarls filling the air as blood soaked the earth. Ryker was relentless, his massive black wolf tearing through the enemy like a storm unleashed. Jessie, Caleb, and Ben fought alongside him, each strike coordinated and lethal.

But even in the midst of the carnage, Ryker's instincts warned him something wasn't right. The vampires fought like they had nothing to lose, as if their focus wasn't entirely on the battle itself.

Jessie, stationed closer to the back lines, had kept a sharp eye on Lara's safety. But when he spotted movement at the far edge of the clearing, his wolf growled low in warning.

"Ryker," Jessie said through the mind-link, his voice tense. "Something's coming."

Jessie's Departure

At the mansion, Lara paced the main hall, her hand pressed over the crescent moon necklace. Her wolf growled softly, restless and uneasy. Every instinct screamed at her to go to the battlefield, but she'd promised Ryker—and Jessie had reinforced that promise before leaving.

Now Jessie stood at the door, his wolf pacing inside him. He turned back to Lara, his expression grim.

"Lara, listen to me," he said, his tone firm. "Whatever happens, no matter what you see or hear, don't open this door."

Lara frowned, her wolf bristling. "What do you mean? Jessie, what's going on?"

"They're trying to draw you out," Jessie said, his voice heavy. "You can't give them what they want. Do you understand me?" Lara hesitated, her hand tightening around the necklace. "Jessie, you're scaring me."

"You need to stay safe," Jessie said. He stepped closer, his tone softening slightly. "Ryker needs you. The pack needs you. Promise me, Lara."

Lara's heart raced, but she nodded slowly. "I promise."

Jessie gave her a small, sad smile. "Good."

Without another word, he slipped out the door and shifted mid-step, his wolf charging toward the battlefield.

The Vampires' Gambit

Back on the battlefield, Ryker and his pack pushed the vampires back toward the tree line. But the battle was far from over.

"Something's wrong," Jessie growled as he joined Ryker's flank. "They're holding back."

Ryker's wolf snarled, his grey eyes scanning the enemy ranks. And then he saw it—a group of vampires emerging from the shadows, dragging two bound figures between them.

His chest tightened as he recognized the terrified faces of Lara's parents.

The Battlefield Freezes

The sight of the bound humans sent a ripple of shock through the pack. Wolves faltered mid-strike, their growls turning into low, warning rumbles as they watched the vampires shove Lara's parents to their knees in the centre of the clearing.

Darius stepped forward; his dark eyes gleaming with triumph. "Well, well," he said, his voice carrying over the battlefield. "It seems we have some unexpected guests."

Ryker shifted back into his human form; his fury barely contained. "Let them go," he growled, his voice low and dangerous.

Darius smirked, taking slow, deliberate steps toward the bound humans. "Oh, I don't think so. They're quite useful, aren't they? After all, how else would I ensure your little mate joins us?"

Ryker growled, his muscles tensing as his wolf bristled beneath the surface. "This isn't their fight."

"But it is now," Darius said, his smirk widening.

Lara's Arrival

From the edge of the battlefield, Jessie's wolf caught the scent of something familiar—something he knew shouldn't be there.

"Lara," he growled softly, turning toward the mansion.

And then he saw her.

Lara stepped into the clearing, her steps steady and unyielding as she moved toward the centre of the battlefield. The crescent moon necklace pulsed faintly against her chest, its glow catching the attention of everyone around her.

"Lara, no!" Jessie barked through the mind-link, his wolf charging toward her.

Ryker turned sharply, his grey eyes blazing with anger. "Lara, get back!"

But it was too late.
Wolves and vampires alike froze as Lara crossed the battlefield, her presence commanding and undeniable. The light from the necklace seemed to catch the edges of her figure, making her appear almost otherworldly as she walked toward the vampires holding her parents.

Her wolf growled softly inside her, its instincts sharpening as she stopped just feet away from Darius.

A Confrontation of Wills

Darius tilted his head, his dark eyes narrowing as he regarded Lara. "So, the white wolf finally shows herself," he said, his voice dripping with mockery. "Come to save Mommy and Daddy?"

"Let them go," Lara said, her voice steady and cold.

Darius smirked, taking a step closer. "And if I don't?"

Lara didn't answer. Her wolf growled low in her chest, its presence steadying her as she met Darius's gaze.

"I wonder," Darius mused, his tone casual. "What would your mate think if you surrendered yourself to save them? Would he hate you for it? Or would he worship you all the more?"

Ryker growled, his voice a low rumble as he stepped closer. "Touch her, and I'll rip your throat out."

Darius chuckled, glancing at Ryker briefly before returning his attention to Lara. “You wolves and your dramatics. So predictable.

A Dangerous Choice

Darius nodded to the vampires holding Lara’s parents, and they shoved the humans forward. Her mother stumbled, her knees hitting the ground hard, while her father struggled against the ropes binding his hands.

“Take them,” Darius said casually. “But know this: the next time we meet, there will be no mercy.”

Lara knelt beside her parents, her wolf growling protectively as the crescent moon necklace pulsed faintly against her chest. Ryker’s wolf moved closer, his grey eyes locking onto Darius with a promise of violence.

But Lara didn’t look at Ryker. Her gaze remained on Darius, her wolf growling low and steady as she whispered, “This isn’t over.”

Chapter 23: The Dawn of Peace

The clearing was electric, the tension between wolves and vampires palpable. Lara stood at the centre, the crescent moon necklace glowing brighter with every passing second. Her parents knelt behind her, bound and trembling, but her focus was elsewhere—on the battle before her, on the power swelling inside her, and on the decision, she had to make.

Her wolf growled softly, its presence steady and grounding. She gripped the necklace instinctively, its heat spreading through her fingers as its glow became blinding.

And then, it happened.

The crescent moon pendant dissolved into shimmering light, the glow surging into her chest. Lara gasped as warmth and power spread through her body, her wolf howling in her mind as it absorbed the energy. Her senses sharpened, the forest around her humming with life, and her wolf surged forward, stronger and more connected than ever before.

The Shift of Power

Lara pressed a hand to her stomach, her breath steadying as she reached out to her wolf. *"Is it safe? Can I do this?"*

Her wolf answered without hesitation. *"Yes. He is safe. We are ready."*

With that reassurance, Lara surrendered to the power. She closed her eyes, letting the transformation take over as her body shifted seamlessly into her wolf form.

She stood taller than ever, her fur glowing with a silvery light that pulsed in time with her heartbeat. Energy radiated from her in waves, spreading through the clearing and silencing the battlefield.

Wolves dropped to their knees, bowing their heads in reverence. Even Ryker's massive black wolf lowered himself, his grey eyes filled with awe and pride.

The vampires froze, their crimson eyes wide with shock. Some stepped back, their faces reflecting a mixture of fear and wonder.

The Speech

Lara raised her head, her glowing eyes locking onto the vampires before her. Her voice, carried through the mind-link and resonating with power, was calm and commanding.

"This ends now," she said, her tone steady and unyielding. "This battle, this hatred—it ends here."

The wolves lifted their heads slightly, their ears perked as they listened. The vampires murmured amongst themselves, their unease growing.

Lara continued, her voice carrying across the clearing. "We are not meant to destroy each other. We are meant to thrive, to protect, to build. But for too long, we have let fear and anger guide us."

She stepped closer to the vampires, her presence radiating strength and empathy. "You are not my enemy. And I am not yours. We have both suffered, both lost. But it doesn't have to be this way. Together, we can end this war. Together, we can rebuild."

Her gaze shifted to the wolves behind her. "Strength is not in how much we destroy. Strength is in how much we create. It is in the bonds we build, the lives we protect, the futures we fight for."

Her eyes locked onto Darius, her voice hardening. "But make no mistake. I will not stand by while my people are threatened. I will protect what is mine, and I will fight for peace. If you want war, you will not win."

The Vampires' Divisions

The vampires glanced nervously at one another, their whispers growing louder. Some of them nodded, their expressions thoughtful, while others clenched their fists, their fear giving way to anger.

"She's right," one vampire said softly, his crimson eyes meeting Lara's. "We've lost too much already."
Another nodded, her voice trembling. "I don't want this anymore."

But Darius stepped forward, his face twisted with disdain. "Fools," he spat. "Do you really think she can save you? She's nothing but a wolf wearing a crown of light."

Lara's wolf growled, her eyes narrowing.

"You're wrong, Darius," she said, her voice steady. "This isn't about me. It's about all of us."

Darius sneered, his hand gesturing toward the vampires who still stood with him. "And what about them? They don't want peace. They want power."

Ryker's Final Stand

Before Darius could say more, Ryker's wolf surged forward, his massive form colliding with the vampire leader. The impact sent shockwaves through the clearing as the two fought, their movements a blur of claws and fangs.

Ryker's growls were deep and relentless, his dominance overpowering. Darius fought viciously, but it was clear he was outmatched.

The remaining vampires who stood with Darius tried to intervene, but the wolves held them back, their unity unshakable. Caleb and Ben tore through the attackers, their wolves moving with precision, while Jessie held the line.

Finally, Ryker's wolf delivered the killing blow, his jaws closing around Darius's throat and snapping it with a brutal finality. The vampire leader crumpled to the ground, lifeless.

The few vampires who had remained loyal to Darius fled into the forest; their resolve broken.

A New Beginning

Lara shifted back into her human form, the glow of her power lingering faintly around her as she approached the vampires who remained.

"You have a choice," she said, her voice soft but firm. "You can leave, or you can join us. But if you choose to stay, it will be as allies, not enemies."

The vampires hesitated, then slowly nodded, their heads dipping in agreement.

One of them stepped forward, a young woman with silver hair and crimson eyes. "We want what you want," she said quietly. "Peace."

Lara nodded, relief washing over her. "Then let's build it together."

Emilia's Leadership

Back at the mansion, Lara descended into the cellar, where Emilia sat quietly, her crimson eyes wide with apprehension.

"It's time," Lara said, extending her hand.

Emilia hesitated before taking it, allowing Lara to lead her outside. The remaining vampires stared at the young girl, their expressions softening as they recognized her.

"She will lead you," Lara said, her voice steady. "She will guide you to a new path. One without war."

Emilia straightened, her fear fading as she stepped forward. "I'll do my best," she said softly.

Lara smiled faintly, her exhaustion finally catching up to her. "I know you will."

The Legends Fulfilled

As the crowd dispersed, Ryker approached Lara, his arms wrapping around her protectively.

"You were incredible," he murmured, his eyes filled with pride.

"I'm tired," Lara admitted, leaning into him.
Ryker chuckled softly, brushing a kiss against her temple. "You've earned it."

The wolves and vampires alike watched her with reverence, their respect clear. Lara was no longer just an alpha—she was a legend, the white wolf who brought peace.

As the stars lit the night sky, Lara allowed herself a moment of quiet, her hand resting on her growing belly. She had fought for her family, her pack, and the future.

And she had won.

Chapter 24: After the Storm

The clearing was quiet now, the echoes of battle fading into the distant sounds of the forest. The air was heavy, charged with the aftermath of what had just transpired. Lara leaned against Ryker, her body trembling with exhaustion but her heart steady with a strange sense of peace.

The vampires lingered at the edge of the clearing, their crimson eyes filled with something new—hope, curiosity, and uncertainty. The wolves stood tall; their forms still tense but no longer bristling with aggression.

This wasn't the end of their journey, Lara realized. It was only the beginning.

A Moment of Respite

Ryker helped Lara back to the mansion, his hand firm around her waist as they walked together. His wolf was calm now, its growls of dominance replaced with quiet pride.

"You should rest," Ryker said softly as they entered their room.

Lara shook her head, though her body screamed for sleep. "There's too much to do. The vampires… the pack…"

"You've done enough for today," Ryker said firmly, cupping her face in his hands. "Let me handle the rest."

Lara met his gaze, her wolf purring softly at the love and strength in his eyes. "Thank you," she whispered, leaning into his touch.

He brushed a kiss against her forehead, then guided her to the bed. "Sleep, Lara. I'll be here when you wake up."

The Aftermath

The pack and the remaining vampires gathered in the mansion's main hall the next day. The tension was still thick, but the hostility had faded. The wolves watched the vampires warily, while the vampires stood close to one another, their movements cautious but cooperative.

Lara entered the room slowly, her presence commanding but not intimidating. The crescent moon necklace was gone now, its power fully absorbed into her, and her aura radiated calm and strength.

"Thank you all for coming," Lara said, her voice steady despite the fatigue that lingered in her body. "We've taken the first step toward peace, but there's more to be done."

She gestured toward Emilia, who stood beside her, her crimson eyes filled with a mix of fear and determination. "This is Emilia. She will lead the vampires going forward."

The vampires exchanged glances, their expressions ranging from surprise to relief.

"She's young," one of them said hesitantly.

"She's strong," Lara countered, her tone firm. "And she understands what it means to lead with compassion. If anyone doubts her, you'll answer to me."

The wolves growled softly in agreement, their loyalty to Lara evident.

Emilia stepped forward, her voice trembling slightly but growing stronger with every word. "I know I have a lot to learn," she said, addressing the vampires. "But I promise to do my best—for all of us. We've lost so much already. It's time to start building something new."

A Fragile Truce

Over the next few days, the wolves and vampires worked together to establish the terms of their truce. Patrols were organized to ensure the safety of both groups, and a neutral meeting place was designated for future discussions.

Lara watched with quiet pride as her pack adapted to the changes. Caleb and Ben took charge of training the younger wolves to work alongside the vampires, while Maeve helped Emilia navigate her new responsibilities.
Ryker was a constant presence at her side, his leadership steady and unyielding as he supported her vision for peace.

"They'll follow you," he said one evening as they sat on the balcony, overlooking the forest. "Wolves and vampires alike. They know you're the future."

Lara leaned into him, her hand resting on her stomach. "I just hope I can live up to their trust."

Ryker kissed her temple, his voice soft but certain. "You already have."

Preparing for New Life

As the days passed, Lara's pregnancy became more pronounced. Her belly grew rounder, and the baby's movements became stronger, each kick a reminder of the new life she was carrying. The pack rallied around her; their excitement palpable. Maeve and the other women organized small gatherings to celebrate the baby, offering Lara advice and sharing stories of their own experiences.

"You're going to be an amazing mother," Kate said one afternoon, her voice filled with warmth.

Lara smiled, her hand resting on her belly. "I hope so."

"You will be," Lilly added, her grin mischievous. "You've already got the protective part down. Now you just need to work on the bedtime stories."

Rebuilding Bonds

The truce with the vampires wasn't without its challenges. There were moments of tension, misunderstandings that threatened to unravel the fragile peace they'd built.

But each time, Lara stepped in, her calm demeanour and empathetic approach diffusing the conflict. She listened to both sides, her words carrying the weight of her power and her desire for unity.

Ryker, too, played a key role, his strength and leadership earning the respect of even the most sceptical vampires. Together, they forged a new path for their people, one built on trust and cooperation.

The Legends Fulfilled

One evening, as the pack gathered around the firepit outside the mansion, Maeve approached Lara with a small, weathered book in her hands.

"I thought you might want to see this," Maeve said, handing the book to her.

Lara opened it carefully, her breath catching as she saw the illustrations inside—depictions of a glowing white wolf standing at the centre of a battlefield, surrounded by wolves and vampires alike.

"It's you," Maeve said softly.

Lara traced the image with her fingers, her heart swelling with a mix of pride and awe. The prophecy had been fulfilled, but she knew this was only the beginning of her journey.

A Well-Deserved Rest

That night, Lara lay in bed, her body heavy with exhaustion but her mind at peace. Ryker lay beside her, his hand resting protectively on her stomach.
"You did it," he murmured, his voice filled with love.

"We did it," Lara corrected, her eyes closing as sleep began to pull her under.

The crescent moon had set, but its light lingered within her, a constant reminder of the strength and love that had brought them to this moment.

As the mansion settled into a quiet calm, Lara allowed herself to rest, knowing she had earned it.

Chapter 25: A New Life Beckons

The days after the battle settled into a fragile peace. The vampires had taken their leave to rebuild their lives under Emilia's leadership, heading back to their coven with a promise of cooperation and mutual respect. While the tension had eased, the memory of what had transpired remained fresh in the minds of both wolves and vampires, a reminder of the delicate path they had chosen.

For Lara, the truce was both a relief and an opportunity to focus on the future—her family's future. She had been restless as of late, her growing belly making even simple tasks feel monumental. She was ready, eager, to welcome the life she carried, though her wolf's constant stirring added to her impatience.

"You're glowing," Ryker said one morning, leaning against the kitchen counter as Lara stood in front of the fridge, scowling at its contents.

She shot him a playful glare. "I'm starving, Ryker. Glowing or not, I can't find anything in here that sounds good."

"Then let's go find something," Ryker said, pushing off the counter and grabbing his keys. "We'll get food and stop by some shops. I know you've been eyeing that baby boutique in town."

Her face softened, a smile spreading across her lips. "You'd do that with me?"

Ryker smirked, pulling her into a gentle kiss. "For you? Always."

Shopping and Laughter

The small town of Kaiapoi was alive with the hum of late-morning activity as Lara and Ryker walked hand in hand down the main street. Her belly was unmistakable now, and the knowing smiles and kind words from strangers warmed her heart.

They wandered into the baby boutique, a charming shop filled with soft pastel colours, tiny clothes, and shelves of baby toys. Lara immediately gravitated toward a display of onesies, holding one up to Ryker.

“Look at this,” she said, grinning as she held up a onesie with the words *Alpha in Training* embroidered on the front.

Ryker chuckled, his eyes crinkling with amusement. “That’s perfect. Get it.”

Lara’s eyes sparkled as she placed it in her basket, moving on to pick out blankets, tiny shoes, and an assortment of baby essentials. Ryker followed her, his gaze warm as he watched her excitement.

“Do you think he’ll have your eyes?” Lara asked suddenly, glancing at him over her shoulder.

Ryker stepped closer, brushing a hand over her cheek. “I think he’ll have the best of both of us.”

Her heart swelled at his words, and she leaned into him, their bond humming softly between them.

Food and Sensuality

After shopping, they stopped at a small café, choosing a table near the window where the sunlight spilled in. Lara ordered

enough food for two people, her hunger insatiable as she eagerly dug in.

Ryker watched her with a mixture of amusement and admiration, his hand resting on hers between bites.

"You're enjoying this, aren't you?" Lara teased, catching his smirk.

"You're adorable when you're eating like it's your last meal," Ryker said, his tone low and teasing.

Lara rolled her eyes, but her cheeks flushed with warmth. "You're impossible."

"I'm yours," he countered, his voice dropping slightly as he leaned closer. His fingers traced the hollow of her collarbone, igniting sparks that made her skin tingle.

The intensity in his grey eyes sent a shiver down her spine, and she swallowed hard, her wolf purring softly.

"We're in public," she murmured, though her voice lacked conviction.
Ryker's lips brushed against her ear; his breath warm against her skin. "Doesn't mean I can't think about what I want to do to you later."

Her cheeks burned, and she quickly changed the subject, though her wolf growled in anticipation.

A Visit to Her Parents

Later that afternoon, Ryker drove Lara to her parents' house, the familiar sight of the cozy home bringing a wave of nostalgia. Her parents were waiting on the porch, their smiles wide as they saw the car pull up.

"Lara!" her mother called, rushing to meet her as she stepped out of the car. "Oh, sweetheart, you're glowing."

Her father wasn't far behind, his warm smile softening as he pulled Lara into a gentle hug. "It's good to see you, kiddo."

Ryker stood back, watching with quiet pride as Lara reunited with her parents.

"Come in, come in," her mother said, ushering them inside. "You must be starving."

Lara laughed, exchanging a glance with Ryker. "Always."

They spent the afternoon catching up, her parents asking endless questions about the baby, the pack, and the truce with the vampires. Lara kept the conversation light, avoiding the heavier details of the battle and focusing on the excitement of the new life she was preparing for.

After dinner, her mother pulled her aside, her eyes filled with emotion.

"You've grown so much, Lara," she said softly. "You've always been strong, but now… now I see a leader. A mother. Someone who will change the world."

Lara's throat tightened, and she hugged her mother tightly. "I'm just trying to do what's right."

Her mother smiled, brushing a strand of hair from her face. "And you are, sweetheart. You always have."

An Intimate Evening

The drive back to the mansion was quiet, the hum of the engine lulling Lara into a state of calm. When they arrived, Ryker

helped her out of the car, his hand lingering on hers as they walked inside.

"You're quiet," he said, his voice soft.

"Just thinking," Lara replied, glancing up at him. "About everything. The baby. The pack. Us."
Ryker's gray eyes darkened slightly, his wolf stirring as he pulled her closer. "What about us?"

Lara smiled faintly, her heart swelling with love. "How lucky I am to have you."

Ryker's lips curved into a slow smile, and he leaned down, brushing a kiss against her forehead. "You're not the only lucky one, Lara."

He led her to their room, the soft glow of the bedside lamp casting warm shadows across the walls. As soon as the door closed, Ryker's hands found her waist, his touch firm but gentle as he pulled her close.
"You drive me crazy, you know that?" he murmured, his lips trailing along her jaw.

Lara's breath hitched, her wolf purring softly as her hands slid up his chest. "You don't make it easy, you know."

Ryker chuckled, his hands moving to cup her face as he kissed her deeply, his intensity making her knees weak. Their bond hummed between them, the connection pulling them closer until there was nothing but the two of them.

"You're mine, Lara," Ryker growled softly, his voice low and possessive.
"And you're mine," she whispered, her eyes locking onto his as their love and desire consumed them.

A Peaceful Moment

Later, as they lay tangled in each other's arms, the weight of the day melted away. Ryker's hand rested on her belly, his fingers tracing gentle circles as they listened to the quiet hum of the mansion.
"I can't wait to meet him," Ryker said softly, his voice filled with wonder.

Lara smiled, her hand covering his. "Me too."

As her eyes drifted shut, she allowed herself to Savor the moment—the calm, the love, and the promise of the future they were building together.

Chapter 26: Countdown to a New Life

The morning sun filtered through the large windows of the mansion, casting soft golden light over the room. Lara sat at the edge of the bed, one hand resting on her round belly as her wolf purred softly in the back of her mind. The baby's movements were more frequent now, little kicks and rolls that reminded her just how close she was to meeting her son.

Ryker entered the room, carrying a tray with breakfast—eggs, toast, and a generous helping of fresh fruit.

"I thought I'd bring you something," he said, placing the tray in front of her. "You need to take it easy today."

Lara smiled, her heart swelling at his thoughtfulness. "You're spoiling me, you know."

"You deserve it," Ryker replied, sitting beside her and placing a hand over hers on her belly.

Just then, the baby kicked, and Ryker chuckled. "Strong like his mother."

"And stubborn like his father," Lara teased, her eyes sparkling.

A Visit to the Doctor

Later that morning, Ryker insisted on accompanying Lara to her appointment with Dr. Elden, the pack's trusted doctor. The small clinic was quiet, its walls adorned with old photographs of past alphas and their families.

Dr. Elden smiled warmly as Lara entered, his kind eyes twinkling. "Ah, Lara. Ryker. Come in. Let's see how things are progressing."

After a quick examination, Dr. Elden leaned back, his expression thoughtful but pleased.

"He's in position and healthy," he said, addressing Lara. "I'd say you're just days away. Maybe less."

Lara's eyes widened, a mix of excitement and nervousness washing over her.

"It's time to take it easy," Dr. Elden continued. "Put your feet up, let the pack handle things, and focus on yourself and the baby. You've done enough, Alpha."

Ryker nodded firmly, his protective instincts kicking in. "You heard him, Lara. No more running around."

Lara rolled her eyes but smiled. "Fine, but you're not allowed to hover too much."

"No promises," Ryker said, smirking.

Catching Up with Jessie

That afternoon, Lara settled into the couch with a mug of tea, grateful for a rare moment of peace. Jessie arrived not long after, his easy smile lighting up the room as he dropped into the chair opposite her.

"Alpha," he greeted with mock formality, earning a laugh from Lara.

"Jessie," she replied, her tone warm. "It's been a while. How are you?"

"Busy," Jessie admitted, leaning back in his chair. "The pack's been keeping me on my toes. But enough about me. How are you feeling?"

“Like a balloon,” Lara said, smiling faintly. “The doctor says it could be any day now.”

Jessie’s expression softened, and he glanced at her belly. “It’s amazing, you know. You’re going to be a great mom.”

“Thank you,” Lara said, her voice quiet but sincere.

She hesitated for a moment before speaking again. “Jessie, there’s something I want to talk to you about.”

His brow furrowed slightly, but he nodded. “Of course. What is it?”

Lara took a deep breath, meeting his gaze. “I want you to have a bigger role in the pack. As one of Ryker’s seconds. And… I want you to be the baby’s godfather.”

Jessie blinked; his expression stunned. “Lara, I—”

“You’ve been one of my closest friends for as long as I can remember,” Lara said, her voice steady. “I trust you, Jessie. I want my son to grow up knowing he has you in his life.”

Jessie’s throat worked as he tried to find the right words. Finally, he nodded, his voice thick with emotion. “I’d be honoured, Lara. Truly.”

Talking It Over with Ryker

That evening, Lara brought the idea to Ryker as they sat together on the balcony, the cool breeze brushing over them.
“I’ve been thinking,” Lara began, glancing at him. “Jessie should be one of your seconds. And I want him to be the baby’s godfather.”

Ryker's expression softened, and he nodded. "I think that's a great idea. Jessie's been loyal to this pack—and to you—his whole life. He deserves the recognition."

Lara smiled, relief washing over her. "Thank you, Ryker. I knew you'd understand."
Ryker pulled her closer, his lips brushing against her temple. "Anything for you, Lara."

A Visit from Old Friends

The following day, Lara's best friends, Kate and Lilly, arrived at the mansion, their excitement palpable as they hugged her tightly.

"Look at you!" Kate exclaimed; her eyes wide. "You're absolutely glowing."

"You're practically ready to pop," Lilly added with a grin.

Lara laughed, her cheeks flushing. "It feels like it. The doctor says it could be any day now."

The three of them settled in the living room, the conversation flowing easily as they caught up. Lara listened intently as her friends' shared updates about their lives, her heart swelling at the happiness in their voices.

Kate leaned forward; her smile mischievous. "So, I have a boyfriend now."
"Finally!" Lilly teased, earning a laugh from both of them.

"And you won't believe this," Lilly added. "I met someone too. He's amazing, Lara. I think this might be the real thing."

Lara's heart warmed as she listened to her friends' stories, their joy a welcome distraction from the recent turmoil. She decided not to update them on the war that had just happened, choosing instead to focus on the moment and the love that surrounded her.

"I'm so happy for both of you," Lara said sincerely. "You deserve this."

Kate smiled; her eyes sparkling. "And you deserve all the happiness in the world, Lara. You're going to be an incredible mom."

An Evening of Gratitude

As the sun dipped below the horizon, Lara sat by the firepit outside, her hands resting on her belly as she watched the flames dance. Ryker joined her, wrapping a blanket around her shoulders before settling beside her.

"You've been quiet," Ryker said, his voice soft.

"Just thinking," Lara replied, glancing at him. "About how lucky I am. To have you. To have Jessie. To have my friends. And soon… to have him."

Ryker smiled, his hand covering hers. "You deserve all of it, Lara. And more."

Lara leaned into him; her heart full. As the stars lit the night sky, she allowed herself a moment of gratitude—for the peace they had fought for, the love they had built, and the future that awaited them.

Chapter 27: The Weight of the Wait

The days grew longer as the final stretch of Lara's pregnancy tested her strength and patience. While the doctor had assured her that the baby was healthy and ready to arrive any day now, Lara found herself feeling more drained with each passing moment.

It started subtly: she struggled to stay awake during her morning tea or found herself skipping meals because nothing seemed appetizing. But soon, even walking from room to room felt like an impossible task.

Her wolf growled softly in the back of her mind, a quiet but constant presence, urging her to rest. Ryker noticed every change, every moment of hesitation in her movements, and his protectiveness only grew.

Ryker Takes Over

"You're not eating enough," Ryker said one evening as they sat in the dining room. He frowned at her untouched plate; his eyes filled with concern.

"I'm not hungry," Lara replied softly, leaning back in her chair. "I'm just… so tired."
"That's not good enough," Ryker growled, his tone firm but not unkind. He stood, crossing the room to kneel in front of her. "You need to eat, Lara. For you and for him."

She sighed, her wolf stirring weakly in agreement. "I'll try."

Ryker cupped her face in his hands, his touch gentle despite the tension in his jaw. "No trying. You will eat. I'll make something myself if I have to."

Lara blinked at him, surprised by the intensity in his tone. "You'd cook?"

"For you? I'd do anything," Ryker said, his voice softening.

Her lips curved into a faint smile. "I'll eat. I promise."

"Good," he said, brushing a kiss against her forehead before returning to his seat.

Wolves in Waiting

The pack noticed the change in their alpha female, and whispers of concern rippled through the ranks. Jessie was the first to approach Ryker about it, his loyalty and worry evident.

"She's been pushing herself too hard," Jessie said, crossing his arms as he stood beside Ryker on the mansion's balcony. "She never stops."

"She doesn't know how to stop," Ryker replied, his voice low. "But she will now. I won't let her do this alone."

"She's lucky to have you," Jessie said after a moment.

Ryker's gaze softened, his thoughts drifting back to Lara. "No. I'm lucky to have her."

Ryker's Protective Instincts

The next day, Ryker went into full protective mode, ensuring that Lara rested as much as possible. He carried her upstairs when she was too tired to climb, made her meals she couldn't refuse, and even enlisted Maeve and the other women to help with anything that might ease her exhaustion.

At first, Lara resisted, her stubbornness flaring.

"I'm not helpless, Ryker," she protested as he insisted on carrying her to the couch.

"No, you're not," he said, his tone calm but unwavering. "You're carrying our son. That's more than enough."

Her wolf purred softly at his words, and Lara sighed, resting her head against his chest. "You're too good to me, you know."

"Not possible," Ryker replied, brushing a kiss against her temple.

A Quiet Evening

That evening, Ryker set up a cozy spot in front of the fire, complete with blankets, pillows, and Lara's favourite tea. He sat beside her; his arm wrapped around her shoulders as they watched the flames dance.

"You're worrying too much," Lara said softly, though her voice lacked its usual strength.
"I have every reason to worry," Ryker replied, his grey eyes fixed on her. "You're exhausted, you're barely eating, and you've been pushing yourself too hard."

Lara sighed, leaning into him. "I just want to be ready. For him. For the pack. For everything."

"You are ready," Ryker said, his voice firm but gentle. "You've done more than enough, Lara. It's time to let me take care of you."

Her heart swelled at his words, and she closed her eyes, her wolf settling as the warmth of his presence washed over her.

A Late-Night Confession

As the fire burned low and the mansion grew quiet, Ryker shifted to face her, his expression serious.

"Lara," he began, his voice low. "You mean everything to me. You know that, right?"

She opened her eyes, meeting his gaze. "Of course I do."
He hesitated, his jaw tightening. "Then promise me you'll let me take care of you. Promise me you'll stop pushing yourself so hard."

Lara reached up, cupping his face in her hands. "I promise, Ryker. I'll rest. I'll let you help me."

His relief was palpable, and he leaned down, pressing a soft but lingering kiss to her lips. "Good. Because I'm not letting you go through this alone."

A Growing Concern

As the night wore on, Lara drifted off to sleep in Ryker's arms, her breathing slow and steady. But Ryker stayed awake, his wolf restless as he watched over her.

He couldn't shake the feeling that something was off—that her exhaustion was more than just the strain of pregnancy.

The crescent moon necklace's absence didn't escape his notice, and he couldn't help but wonder if its power, now fused with Lara, was taking more of a toll than they realized.
Ryker's jaw tightened as he pulled Lara closer, his protective instincts surging. Whatever was happening, he would figure it out.

Chapter 28: Preparing for the Unknown

The days following Lara's promise to rest were quiet, but Ryker's worry never faded. He was always nearby, ensuring she ate, slept, and stayed comfortable. While Lara appreciated his care, she could sense the unease behind his grey eyes. He was trying to hide it, but her wolf felt it too—a subtle but persistent tension that kept him on edge.

For Lara, the exhaustion lingered like a heavy fog, making even simple tasks feel monumental. Her wolf was quieter than usual, though it stirred now and then, nudging her to trust in their bond.

A Concern Grows

Ryker stood in the mansion's study late one evening, staring at the map of their territory spread across the desk. He wasn't thinking about the pack's patrols or the truce with the vampires. His mind was on Lara—her exhaustion, her sudden loss of appetite, and the weight of her growing power.

Jessie entered the room, his expression curious. "Ryker? What's going on?"

Ryker sighed, running a hand through his hair. "It's Lara. Something doesn't feel right."

Jessie frowned, leaning against the desk. "She's close to giving birth, right? Maybe it's just the strain."

"Maybe," Ryker said, though his tone lacked conviction. "But it's more than that. Ever since the necklace fused with her, she's been different. Stronger, yes, but also… drained."

Jessie nodded thoughtfully. "What are you thinking?"

"I'm thinking I need answers," Ryker replied, his jaw tightening. "And I'm not waiting until something happens to find them."

Lara's Conversation with Her Wolf

The following morning, Lara sat on the edge of her bed, her hands resting on her belly. The baby's movements were strong, but her body felt weaker than ever. She closed her eyes, reaching out to her wolf.

"What's happening to me?" she asked, her voice trembling in her mind.

Her wolf stirred; its growl soft but steady. *"You're carrying more than just the baby, Lara. You carry the power of the crescent moon."*

"Is it hurting me?" Lara asked, her heart tightening.

"No," her wolf replied firmly. *"But it's testing you. The necklace's power is ancient, and it's learning you as much as you are learning it. You're not just carrying a child—you're carrying your future as alpha, and the balance must be found."*

Lara took a deep breath, her wolf's words settling over her like a heavy blanket. *"Will I be ready when he comes?"*

"You are ready," her wolf assured her. *"And I am with you."*

Ryker Seeks Answers

Later that day, Ryker called on Maeve, the pack's historian and one of its oldest members. She met him in the library, her sharp eyes narrowing as he explained his concerns.

"Lara's power is immense," Maeve said, her voice calm but thoughtful. "The crescent moon chose her, but it didn't come without cost. Power like that doesn't simply exist—it must settle, grow, and become part of the one who wields it."

"And what does that mean for her?" Ryker asked, his voice tight.

"It means she's adapting," Maeve replied. "Her body, her mind, her wolf—they're all learning to balance the power she now holds. It's exhausting, but it's not harming her. If anything, it's preparing her for what's to come."

Ryker's jaw clenched, his protective instincts flaring. "So, there's nothing I can do to help her?"
Maeve's gaze softened. "You're already helping her, Ryker. You're her mate, her partner, her strength. She needs you now more than ever."

A Quiet Night Together

That evening, Ryker prepared a small dinner for Lara, keeping the portions light but filling. She sat at the kitchen table, watching him with a mixture of amusement and affection as he moved around the kitchen.

"You're getting good at this," Lara teased, her smile faint but genuine.

"Don't get used to it," Ryker replied, smirking as he set the plate in front of her.

Lara laughed softly, though it quickly turned into a yawn. Ryker's expression grew serious, and he knelt beside her, his hand covering hers.

"You're going to be okay, Lara," he said firmly. "We're going to get through this."

Lara nodded, her throat tightening as tears welled in her eyes. "I know. It's just… a lot."

Ryker reached up, brushing a tear from her cheek. "You're not alone. Remember that." Lara leaned into his touch, her heart swelling with love. "Thank you, Ryker. For everything."

A Sudden Burst of Energy

The next morning, Lara woke feeling surprisingly refreshed. Her wolf purred softly; its presence stronger than it had been in

days. She stretched slowly, her hand resting on her belly as the baby kicked with more vigour than ever.

She smiled faintly, murmuring, “You’re strong, little one. Just like your dad.”

Ryker entered the room moments later; his brow furrowed with concern that eased the moment he saw her expression.

“You look… better,” he said cautiously.

“I feel better,” Lara admitted, her voice soft. “I think I needed the rest. And… I think the baby’s almost ready.”

Ryker’s grey eyes softened, and he stepped closer, placing a hand over hers on her belly. “We’re almost there.”

A Moment of Reflection

That evening, Lara and Ryker sat on the balcony, watching the sun dip below the horizon. The forest was quiet, its energy peaceful, as if the world itself was holding its breath.

“I’ve been thinking,” Lara said, her voice steady. Ryker glanced at her, his brow lifting slightly. “About what?”

"About the pack. About the baby. About everything," Lara replied. She turned to face him, her eyes shining with determination. "We've come so far, Ryker. And we've done it together. I know I've been tired, and I know I've scared you, but I'm not afraid anymore. I'm ready for whatever comes next."

Ryker's heart swelled at her words, and he leaned forward, brushing his lips against hers in a kiss that was soft but filled with promise. "You've always been ready, Lara. And I'll always be here for you."

Lara smiled, her hand resting on his cheek. "I love you, Ryker."

"And I love you," he murmured, his voice low and steady.

As the stars began to appear in the night sky, Lara allowed herself to savour the moment—the love, the calm, and the promise of the future they were building together.

Chapter 29: The Arrival

The day began like any other. The soft glow of dawn filtered through the mansion's tall windows, illuminating the quiet stillness of the home. Lara had woken early, the baby's movements unusually active, as if her son was trying to break free. She placed her hand on her belly, smiling faintly as she felt his kicks.

"Today's the day, isn't it?" she whispered softly to herself.

Her wolf stirred in agreement; its presence calm but steady. *"It's time."*

The air carried a faint coolness, laced with the earthy scent of the forest after an early morning drizzle. The house itself was quiet, with only the faint murmurs of the pack waking and preparing for the day echoing from the lower floors.

Ryker was already up, his silhouette visible through the doorway as he leaned against the balcony railing, the cool breeze tousling his hair. He turned when he heard Lara stirring, his grey eyes softening with warmth.
"Good morning, love," he said, stepping back inside. "How are you feeling?"

Lara smiled faintly, though a flicker of discomfort crossed her face. "Like he's ready to meet us."

Ryker's brows furrowed, and he moved to her side, his hand immediately resting on her belly. "How strong are the contractions?"

"They're… starting," Lara admitted.

The First Signs

As the morning progressed, the contractions became more consistent, pulling her deeper into the realization that her son's arrival was imminent. The pack buzzed with quiet anticipation as Ryker alerted Dr. Elden, who arrived swiftly, his bag of supplies in hand.
The main bedroom was prepared with care. A low table by the window held a steaming pot of herbal tea Maeve had brewed specifically for Lara, its faint scent of chamomile and lavender mingling with the fresh pine of the forest wafting through the open window.

Thick blankets were folded neatly on a chair near the bed, and a basin of warm water rested on a small stand nearby, its surface reflecting the soft amber light of the room.

Lara sat on the edge of the bed; her breathing measured but strained as another contraction gripped her. Ryker knelt beside her, his large hand enveloping hers, his thumb rubbing soothing circles on her knuckles.

"You're doing great," he murmured, his voice low and steady.

Lara managed a small smile, though her grip on his hand tightened. "This is… harder than I thought it would be."

"You've handled worse," Ryker said, his lips curving into a faint smirk. "And you're stronger than anything that's come your way."

Dr. Elden's Observations

Dr. Elden stood at the foot of the bed, his weathered face calm but focused as he took notes on a small pad. His sharp eyes flicked between Lara and his medical tools, his mind clearly working through more than just the present moment.

“Alpha,” he said, addressing Ryker, “I’ve been reviewing some older texts about the crescent moon necklace and its power.”

Ryker’s attention snapped to him, his grey eyes narrowing. “What did you find?”

Dr. Elden hesitated, his gaze shifting to Lara. “It’s nothing to be alarmed about yet. But it’s possible that the necklace’s energy, now fused with Lara, may be influencing the child’s development. It’s likely why this labour is progressing slower than normal.”

“What does that mean?” Lara asked, her voice strained but steady.

“It means your son may inherit more than just strength,” Dr. Elden said carefully. “The necklace’s power is ancient and vast, and some of it may have been passed to him. He could be… extraordinary.”

Lara’s wolf growled softly, its presence bolstering her resolve. “He’ll be fine,” she said firmly.

Dr. Elden nodded, though his expression remained serious. “We’ll proceed as we would with any birth. But I’ll keep a close watch.”

Hours of Waiting

As the labour stretched into the afternoon, the atmosphere in the room shifted. The once-gentle contractions became sharper, their intensity pulling strained groans from Lara’s lips. Ryker stayed at her side, his hand never leaving hers, his face etched with a mix of worry and determination.

"Breathe, Lara," he reminded her softly, his voice steady. "Just breathe."

She nodded, her breathing ragged as she leaned forward, her forehead resting against his shoulder. The earthy scent of his skin grounded her, a reminder of his unwavering presence.

The pack waited outside the room, their low murmurs blending with the occasional howl that carried from the forest. Maeve had joined the others, her calming presence ensuring the wolves stayed patient and respectful.

Inside, the tension grew. The smell of lavender from the tea pot now mingled with the faint tang of sweat in the warm air, a testament to Lara's effort.

A Shift in Energy

By early evening, the room felt charged, as though the air itself was alive with an unseen force. Lara's wolf stirred more frequently now, its growls louder in her mind.

"He's almost here," it said, its tone steady but urgent.

Dr. Elden moved to her side; his hands deft but gentle as he checked her progress. His face remained calm, though there was a flicker of something else curiosity, maybe even awe.

"The baby is descending," he announced, his voice carrying an undertone of relief. "We're close now."

Ryker pressed a kiss to Lara's damp forehead, his thumb brushing away a stray tear. "You're amazing," he whispered. "You're so strong, Lara."

Her breaths were shallow, her chest rising and falling quickly as another contraction gripped her. “I’m ready,” she gasped, her wolf’s growls mixing with her own voice.

The Final Push Begins

The room seemed smaller now, the world narrowing to the space between Lara and Ryker as she prepared for the final stage of labour. Dr. Elden positioned himself at the foot of the bed, his hands steady and his voice calm as he guided her.

“On the next contraction, Lara, I want you to push with everything you’ve got,” he instructed.

The contraction came like a wave, crashing through her with a force that stole her breath. She gripped Ryker’s hand tightly, her knuckles white as she bore down, her wolf lending its strength.

The room was filled with the sound of her effort, Ryker’s soothing words, and Dr. Elden’s calm instructions.

“That’s it, Lara,” Dr. Elden said, his voice steady. “You’re doing beautifully. I can see the head.”

Tears filled Ryker’s eyes as he leaned closer, his lips brushing against her ear. “You’ve got this. I’m here. I’m not going anywhere.”

As the sun dipped below the horizon, casting a golden glow through the window, the energy in the room reached its peak. The scent of pine and earth from the forest mingled with the warm air, wrapping around Lara like a comforting embrace.

Dr. Elden’s voice was calm but firm as he said, “One more push, Lara. Just one more.”

Lara took a deep breath, her body trembling as she gathered every ounce of strength she had left. Her wolf howled in her mind, its voice blending with her own as she pushed with everything she had.

And then, a sound broke through the tension—a sharp, clear cry that filled the room and sent a wave of relief crashing over everyone.

“He’s here,” Dr. Elden said, his voice soft with awe.

Ryker’s face broke into a grin, tears spilling freely as he pressed a kiss to Lara’s temple. “You did it, love. He’s perfect.”

But as Dr. Elden carefully lifted the baby, his brow furrowed slightly, his gaze flicking to Lara. “There’s… something about him,” he said, his voice cautious. “Something extraordinary.”

Lara, too exhausted to respond, let her eyes flutter shut, her heart filled with love and relief as the baby’s cries echoed in her ears.

Chapter 30: The Light of the Moon

The moment the baby's cry pierced the room, time seemed to stop. The sounds of the forest faded into silence, and the hum of life that filled the mansion stilled, as if even nature itself was holding its breath. Lara's chest rose and fell with deep, laboured breaths, her body trembling from exhaustion. The warmth of Ryker's hand on hers was the only thing tethering her to the present as the weight of what she had just accomplished washed over her.

The soft, newborn cry filled the room again, clearer this time, like music that brought life back into the world.

"He's here," Dr. Elden said softly, lifting the baby into view, his tone filled with awe. "He's perfect."

The First Glimpse

Lara forced her eyes open, her body aching but her heart racing with anticipation. She craned her neck, desperate to see her son. The glow that had enveloped her during labour now seemed to have transferred to the tiny being in Dr. Elden's hands.
The baby glowed faintly, a subtle, silvery light that shimmered softly around his skin. His hair was thick and dark, curling slightly at the edges, a stark contrast to the pale blue of his wide, curious eyes that blinked up at the world for the first time.

"He's glowing," Ryker whispered, his voice filled with reverence.

Dr. Elden's hands trembled slightly as he wrapped the baby in a soft, cream-colored blanket, careful not to extinguish the glow that emanated from him. "This child," he murmured, his voice barely above a whisper, "is unlike any I've seen."

Lara reached out instinctively, her arms aching with the need to hold her son. Dr. Elden stepped closer, gently placing the baby in her arms.
The moment their skin touched, the glow around the baby intensified for just a heartbeat, as though it recognized its source. Lara gasped softly, her wolf stirring with joy and awe in the back of her mind.

"He's beautiful," she whispered, tears streaming down her face.

A Mother's Love

The baby nestled into her arms, his tiny fingers curling instinctively around the edge of the blanket. His blue eyes blinked slowly, peering up at her with a calm curiosity that took her breath away.

"Hi, little one," Lara said softly, her voice trembling. She brushed a finger across his chubby cheek, marvelling at the warmth of his skin and the softness of his hair.

Her heart swelled with an intensity she had never known before, a love so powerful it felt as though it might break her apart. Tears blurred her vision, but she didn't look away, unable to stop staring at the tiny miracle she held in her arms.

"You're perfect," she murmured, her voice catching. "Absolutely perfect."

Her wolf growled softly in agreement, its presence strong and steady, radiating pride and joy.

A Father's Pride

Ryker's hand rested on Lara's shoulder as he leaned closer, his grey eyes shimmering with unshed tears. He stared at the baby as though he were witnessing the moon itself descend to earth.

"He's incredible," Ryker whispered, his voice filled with awe.

The baby stirred slightly, his tiny lips parting as a soft, almost musical coo escaped him. Ryker's chest tightened, his wolf growling with fierce protectiveness.

Lara glanced up at him, her own tears spilling freely. "He's yours, Ryker. He looks just like you."

Ryker chuckled softly, brushing a hand over the baby's thick, dark hair. "He has your eyes," he said, his voice shaking. "And your light."

The words hung between them, filled with a meaning only they understood. Ryker leaned down, pressing a kiss to Lara's temple before gently touching the baby's cheek with a finger.

"Welcome to the world, little one," he murmured. "You've already made it better."

The Crescent Moon Mark

As Lara shifted the blanket to get a better look at her son, her breath caught. Nestled just beneath his collarbone, faint but unmistakable, was the shape of a crescent moon.

"Ryker," she said, her voice trembling as she looked up at him.

He followed her gaze, his grey eyes widening as he saw the mark. It shimmered faintly, as though it carried its own light, a mirror to the glow that surrounded the baby.

Dr. Elden stepped closer, his brows furrowing as he examined the mark. "A crescent moon," he said softly, his voice laced with awe. "This is no ordinary birthmark."

"It's the necklace," Ryker said, his tone firm. "The power Lara absorbed—it's in him."

Lara's wolf growled in agreement; its voice steady in her mind. *"He is pure. The purest of pure."*

"He's meant for something greater," Dr. Elden said, his gaze lingering on the mark. "This child… he will be a leader unlike any we've seen."

A Bigger Miracle

The baby yawned, the softest sound escaping him as his tiny fists stretched and flexed. His size was remarkable—larger than any pup Lara had heard of, but not unnaturally so. He was healthy, strong, and perfect.

"He's bigger than I expected," Lara said softly, marvelling at his weight in her arms.

Dr. Elden nodded. "He's a true alpha, in every sense. His strength will become clear as he grows."

Ryker's hand slid to Lara's back; his voice filled with pride. "He'll be everything this pack needs. Everything we've dreamed of."

Joy and Mystery

The room seemed to hold its breath again as Lara cradled her son, the soft glow of the baby casting a warm light on her face. Ryker sat beside her, his arm wrapped protectively around her shoulders, the weight of their journey finally settling over them.

“I didn’t know I could love someone so much,” Lara said softly, her tears continuing to fall.

Ryker kissed her cheek, his own voice heavy with emotion. “He’s our everything, Lara. Just like you’re mine.”

The baby stirred again, his tiny hand brushing against Lara’s chest. The crescent moon mark shimmered faintly, a reminder of the power that had brought them to this moment.

As they stared at their son, the enormity of what they had created settled over them. He was more than a child. He was a symbol of hope, strength, and the future they had fought so hard to build.

The Pack Reacts

Outside the room, the pack waited in tense silence, their ears perked and their wolves restless. When the faint sound of a baby’s cry reached them, a collective sigh of relief rippled through the group.

Maeve turned to Jessie, her sharp eyes softening. “He’s here.”

Jessie nodded, his own wolf settling. “And the world just changed.”

The First Night

As the moon rose high in the sky, Lara and Ryker remained in the room, the world outside forgotten. The baby slept peacefully in Lara's arms, his glow dimming slightly but never fading.

Lara leaned against Ryker, her exhaustion finally catching up with her. "He's perfect," she murmured, her voice heavy with sleep.

Ryker kissed the top of her head, his hand resting over hers on the baby. "He is. Just like his mother."

As the baby shifted slightly, his crescent moon mark glimmered faintly in the moonlight streaming through the window. It was a reminder of the journey that had brought them here and the future that awaited them.

In that moment, everything felt right.

Chapter 31: A Life of Love and Celebration

The days following the birth of Lara and Ryker's son passed in a haze of love and wonder. The mansion, usually abuzz with activity, seemed to settle into a peaceful rhythm, as if the world itself had paused to honour the arrival of the new alpha heir.

In the master suite, Lara and Ryker cocooned themselves with their newborn, their focus solely on their tiny, glowing miracle.

A Sanctuary of Love

The room, now a sanctuary, carried the unmistakable warmth of new life. The air was tinged with the faint, sweet scent of the newborn—soft and delicate, like fresh linens kissed by morning dew. The glow of the baby's presence lingered faintly, a subtle shimmer that seemed to make the room brighter and more alive.

Near the bed, a beautiful white bassinet stood draped with sheer, cream-colored fabric, its edges embroidered with tiny crescent moons. A matching changing table stood against the far wall, its surface lined with soft, plush covers. Stacks of tiny, folded clothes, blankets, and diapers were arranged neatly on nearby shelves, their pastel tones adding to the room's tranquil ambiance.

The baby, bundled snugly in a soft navy blanket, lay in Lara's arms as she rocked gently in a chair by the window. The soft cooing sounds he made melted her heart, and her wolf purred in satisfaction at every tiny noise and movement he made.

Ryker sat close, his eyes fixed on them, filled with so much love and pride that it made Lara's breath catch every time she glanced his way.

A Mother's Joy

"I can't stop looking at him," Lara said softly, brushing her thumb over the baby's soft cheek.

Ryker reached out, his hand resting over hers. "Neither can I. He's… perfect."

The baby stirred slightly, yawning and stretching his tiny fingers, and Lara couldn't help but laugh, the sound light and filled with joy.

"He's so pure," she murmured, her voice trembling slightly. "I can feel it, Ryker. He's good. So, so good." Ryker leaned closer, pressing a kiss to her temple. "That's because he's yours, Lara. Your heart, your light. And ours."

Her eyes filled with tears, and she smiled, her voice a whisper. "I've never loved anyone like this." "Me neither," Ryker admitted, his voice thick. He gently took the baby from her arms, cradling him against his chest.

The sight of Ryker holding their son made Lara's chest swell with emotion. His large hands seemed impossibly gentle as he stroked the baby's dark hair, his lips brushing against the soft crown of his head.

Healing and Happiness

Lara healed faster than she had anticipated. Within days, her strength had returned, and her appetite had come back with a vengeance. The kitchen staff kept sending up trays of food, from warm soups and freshly baked bread to platters of sweet treats that made her laugh with delight.

"You're eating for two now," Ryker teased one evening as she finished her second helping of stew.

"I think it's more like three," Lara replied, grinning.

Her laughter filled the room often, a sound that had been missing for far too long. The bond between her and Ryker grew even deeper in these quiet days, their shared love for their son strengthening the already unbreakable connection they had.

The Pack's Dedication

While Lara and Ryker spent their days focused on their newborn, Jessie and the pack stepped up to ensure everything ran smoothly. Patrols were well-organized, the territory was secured, and the pack members worked together seamlessly under Jessie's leadership.

"I've got everything covered," Jessie assured Ryker during a brief check-in. "You just focus on your family."

Ryker clapped Jessie on the shoulder, his gratitude evident. "Thank you, Jessie. I couldn't ask for a better second."

Jessie grinned. "Just wait until I start spoiling that little guy. He's going to grow up thinking his godfather is the coolest wolf in the pack."

A Night to Celebrate

After days of peace and quiet, the pack decided it was time to celebrate properly. Maeve suggested a fiesta in the grand hall, a gathering that would honour the new alpha heir and bring everyone together in joy and unity.

The grand hall was transformed into a magical space. Long tables were adorned with flowing white tablecloths and vases filled with fresh flowers from the forest. Strings of twinkling lights crisscrossed the ceiling, casting a warm glow over the room. The scent of roasted meats, spiced stews, and freshly baked bread filled the air, mingling with the laughter and chatter of the pack as they arrived in their best attire.

Lara and Ryker stood just outside the hall; their son bundled in Ryker's arms as they prepared to make their entrance.
"Are you ready?" Ryker asked, his voice low and warm.

Lara adjusted the soft shawl draped over her shoulders, her hand resting lightly on Ryker's arm. "More than ready."

The Announcement

The room fell silent as the alphas entered, all eyes turning toward the tiny bundle in Ryker's arms. A collective gasp rippled through the pack as they noticed the faint glow surrounding the baby, the crescent moon mark visible on his chest where the blanket had shifted slightly.

Ryker stepped forward, his voice steady and commanding. "Tonight, we celebrate the future of this pack. Our son, the next alpha, has arrived. He is strong. He is pure. And he is ours."

Lara smiled, her voice filled with warmth as she added, "We want to introduce you all to our son, *Kael Ryker Wolfe*."

The name rang through the hall, its strength and power undeniable.

The room erupted into cheers, howls echoing off the walls as the pack welcomed their new heir with overwhelming joy.

Dancing and Laughter

The fiesta was filled with life and love. Wolves laughed and danced, their voices blending with the music that filled the hall. Lara and Ryker sat at the head table, Kael nestled comfortably in his bassinet beside them, his tiny chest rising and falling with soft, even breaths.

Maeve approached with a glass of sparkling cider, her eyes twinkling as she raised it in a toast. "To the future," she said, her voice steady. "To Kael."

The pack echoed her words, their glasses raised high as they celebrated the promise of a new generation.

A Moment Alone

As the night wound down, Lara and Ryker slipped away from the crowd, retreating to the balcony that overlooked the forest. The cool night air brushed against their skin as they stood together, Kael cradled in Lara's arms.

The stars were bright above them, their light soft and soothing as they gazed out at the quiet expanse of trees.

"He's everything I ever dreamed of," Lara said softly, her voice filled with wonder. Ryker wrapped an arm around her shoulders, his lips brushing against her temple. "And you're everything I ever dreamed of." Lara smiled, leaning into him as Kael shifted slightly, letting out a soft coo.

"We're so lucky," Lara murmured, her voice heavy with emotion.

"No," Ryker said, his voice steady. "We're not lucky. We're blessed."

As they stood together under the stars, their hearts full, they knew that this was only the beginning of the beautiful life they were building together.

Chapter 32: A New Era and New Suspicions

The days after the fiesta settled into a warm, happy rhythm. The pack buzzed with excitement over Kael's arrival, and Lara and Ryker continued to stay cocooned in their private space, cherishing every moment with their son. The mansion, a hub of activity during the day, was filled with laughter, the occasional howl of celebration, and the sweet scent of pine and wildflowers drifting in through the open windows.

But life didn't pause for long. Lara's parents and her closest friends had arranged to visit, eager to meet the new alpha heir and share in the joy. While the visits brought warmth and excitement, Lara and Ryker's wolves remained on high alert, sensing that something was not quite right about one of the visitors.

The Morning Routine

The master suite had fully transformed into a nursery for Kael. Sunlight streamed through the large windows, casting a golden glow over the room. The white bassinet still stood near the bed, now flanked by stacks of diapers, toys, and soft blankets gifted by pack members. The scent of Kael—fresh, warm, and sweet—filled the room, making it feel like a sanctuary.

Kael cooed happily as Lara changed him on the padded table near the wall. His tiny legs kicked energetically, and she couldn't help but laugh as she leaned down to press a kiss to his soft, dark hair.

"You're the sweetest thing," Lara whispered, her voice filled with awe.

Behind her, Ryker leaned against the doorframe, arms crossed, a small smile on his face. "He takes after his mother."

Lara turned, rolling her eyes but smiling. "He takes after both of us. Look at this hair—it's all you."

Ryker walked over, placing a hand on Kael's tiny belly and making a soft growling sound that sent the baby into a fit of giggles. "That's my boy," Ryker murmured, his voice filled with pride.

A Welcomed Visit

Later that morning, Lara's parents arrived, their car pulling up the long driveway. Her mother stepped out first, her face lighting up when she saw Lara standing on the porch with Kael in her arms.

"Lara!" she called, hurrying up the steps. "Oh, sweetheart, let me see him!"

Lara laughed, gently handing Kael over to her mother, who cradled him as though he were the most precious thing in the world.

"He's beautiful," her mother whispered, tears in her eyes.

Her father joined them, his expression softening as he placed a hand on Lara's shoulder. "You did good, kiddo."

Ryker stepped forward, shaking her father's hand firmly. "Welcome back. We've got everything set up for you inside."

As they entered the mansion, the room filled with warmth and laughter. Her parents doted on Kael, marvelling at his tiny hands and the soft glow that seemed to linger around him.

Preparations for Dinner

As evening approached, the mansion's kitchen came alive with activity. The staff prepared a feast, filling the air with the mouthwatering scents of roasted meats, seasoned vegetables, and freshly baked bread.

Lara and her friends moved to the dining room, where the table was set with fine China and flickering candles. Kael rested in a bassinet near the table, his tiny form glowing faintly even in sleep.

But as the group gathered, Lara noticed Logan's eyes lingering on the baby longer than necessary. Her wolf stirred uneasily; its growl low but insistent.

"Everything okay?" Ryker asked through their bond, his voice steady but concerned.
"I don't know yet," Lara replied silently. "But I'm watching him."

Secrets Revealed

As the meal progressed, Logan grew quieter, his eyes darting toward the windows as though he were looking for something—or someone. Lara exchanged a glance with Ryker, her wolf growling louder now.

Finally, Logan cleared his throat, leaning forward slightly. "You've built quite the life here," he said, his tone casual but laced with something Lara couldn't quite place.

"We're proud of it," Ryker replied, his grey eyes sharp.

Logan's gaze flicked to Kael, then back to Lara. "And your son… he's special, isn't he?"

The room fell silent, the tension palpable. Lara's heart raced as her wolf bristled, ready to protect what was hers.
"Everyone is special in their own way," Lara said carefully, her tone calm but edged.

Logan's smile didn't reach his eyes as he leaned back. "Of course."

The unease in the room was undeniable now, and as Lara's wolf growled louder in her mind, she knew this was far from over.

Chapter 33: Hidden Truths and Heated Teasing

The dining room was quiet after Logan's offhand comment, his words lingering in the air like an unwelcome shadow. Lara's wolf growled softly in her mind, its unease sharpening her instincts. She glanced at Ryker, who sat at her side, his expression unreadable but his posture tense.

Kael stirred faintly in his bassinet, the soft glow surrounding him pulsing as though responding to the charged energy in the room.

Lara turned her attention back to Logan, her voice calm but firm. "What exactly do you mean by 'special,' Logan?"

Logan smiled faintly, his shoulders shrugging in an attempt to appear casual. "I just mean… look at him. There's something about him, isn't there? Something… different."

"He's our son," Ryker said, his tone steady but edged with authority. "That's all you need to know."

The tension was thick, but before Logan could respond, Kate interjected with a light laugh, her voice cutting through the heavy silence.

"Logan's just curious," she said, her smile strained as she placed a hand on his arm. "He didn't mean anything by it."

Lara forced a smile, though her wolf growled low in her chest. "Of course. Let's enjoy dinner."

Unspoken Worries

After the meal, Lara and Ryker retreated to their room with Kael, leaving Jessie to keep an eye on their guests. The moment the door closed behind them, Ryker turned to her, his grey eyes dark with concern.

"There's something off about him," he said, his voice low but firm. "I don't like the way he was looking at Kael."

Lara nodded, placing Kael gently into his bassinet. "I felt it too. My wolf hasn't stopped growling since they arrived."

Ryker crossed the room, his movements sharp with tension. "I don't trust him, Lara. He knows more than he's letting on."

"Then we figure out what he's hiding," Lara said, her voice steady despite the unease twisting in her chest.

Ryker's gaze softened slightly as he stepped closer, his hands resting on her shoulders. "You're amazing, you know that?"

Lara smiled faintly, leaning into his touch. "I'm just doing what's best for our family."

His lips curved into a small smirk, and he lowered his voice to a near-growl. "Still. You drive me crazy."

Sensual Teasing

Lara tilted her head, her wolf purring softly at the shift in Ryker's tone. "Do I now?"

"You have no idea," Ryker murmured, his hands sliding down her arms and settling on her waist. He pulled her closer, his breath warm against her ear.

Her heart raced, a blush creeping up her neck as his lips brushed against her skin. "Ryker," she whispered, her voice soft but warning.

His smirk widened, his fingers pressing gently into her hips as he leaned down, his grey eyes locking onto hers. "What? I'm not doing anything."

Lara arched a brow, her lips twitching into a small smile. "You're impossible."
"And you love it," he replied, his voice a low rumble.

She laughed softly, her hands resting on his chest as she pushed him back slightly. "You're lucky I do."

Ryker chuckled, his hands lingering on her waist before he stepped back, his eyes glinting with playful dominance. "Go check on Kael before I decide I don't want to stop."

Lara's cheeks burned as she turned toward the bassinet, her wolf growling softly in approval. "You're incorrigible," she said over her shoulder.

"And you're mine," Ryker countered, his smirk lingering as he leaned against the edge of the bed.

Unravelling Secrets

The following morning, Lara and Ryker convened with Jessie in the study, the soft scent of pine and leather filling the room.

Jessie leaned against the desk; his arms crossed as he listened to Ryker recount the events of the previous evening.

"There's something about Logan," Ryker said, his voice low. "He's hiding something. The way he was looking at Kael… it wasn't curiosity. It was something else."

Jessie nodded; his expression serious. "I've been keeping an eye on him. He doesn't act like a typical human. There's something in the way he moves, the way he watches people. It's calculated."

Lara frowned, her wolf growling softly. "Then we need to figure out what he is—and what he wants."

Jessie straightened, his jaw tightening. "I'll start digging. There's got to be something about him we can use."

Ryker nodded; his grey eyes hard. "Do it. And keep him away from Kael."

A Suspicious Discovery

Later that day, Jessie returned with news. He found Lara and Ryker in the nursery, where Kael lay cooing happily in his bassinet, his tiny fingers grasping at the air.

"Logan's name isn't real," Jessie said bluntly, his voice quiet but firm. "I found records of someone matching his description in another pack's territory. He disappeared about two years ago—right around the time their alpha was killed."

Ryker's jaw tightened, his wolf growling low in his chest. "What else did you find?"

Jessie hesitated, glancing at Lara. "He's not just a human, Lara. I think he's something… else."

Lara's stomach tightened, her hand instinctively moving to rest on Kael's bassinet. "What do you mean?"
Jessie sighed; his voice grim. "I don't know yet. But whatever he is, he's dangerous."

A Confrontation Brewing

That evening, Logan wandered the mansion's grounds, his posture relaxed but his eyes sharp as they scanned the forest's edge. Lara watched him from the balcony, her wolf bristling as she observed his movements.

"He's looking for something," Ryker said quietly, stepping up behind her.

"Or someone," Lara replied, her voice steady but cold.

As Logan turned back toward the mansion, his gaze flicked up toward the balcony, meeting Lara's eyes for a brief moment. A faint smile crossed his lips, but it didn't reach his eyes.

"We need to act," Ryker said, his tone firm.

Lara nodded, her hand tightening on the railing. "And we will. But not yet. Let him think he's safe."

Her wolf growled softly in agreement; its voice filled with quiet resolve. *"We'll protect what's ours."*

Chapter 34: A Betrayal Unfolds

The quiet of early morning settled over the mansion like a soft blanket. The air was cool and crisp, the first hints of dawn spilling across the horizon. Lara stirred in bed, the faint cries of Kael pulling her from a light sleep.

Ryker was already awake, standing by the window with his arms crossed as he surveyed the forest below. His wolf was restless, a low growl humming at the back of his mind.

"Something doesn't feel right," he said softly, turning to glance at Lara as she picked up Kael from his bassinet.

"You've been saying that for days," Lara replied, her voice soothing as she cradled Kael in her arms. She kissed the top of his head, inhaling the sweet, comforting scent of her newborn. "But we're safe here, Ryker. The pack is on high alert. Nothing is going to happen."

Ryker's grey eyes darkened slightly, his jaw tightening. "I don't trust Logan."
"Neither do I," Lara admitted. "But we're keeping him close for a reason. Jessie is watching him."

The Call

Their conversation was interrupted by the sharp ring of Ryker's phone. He frowned, pulling it from his pocket and glancing at the screen. It was one of the pack members stationed at the border.

"This early?" Ryker muttered before answering. "What is it?"

The voice on the other end was shaky, almost frantic. "Alpha, there's been an accident."

Ryker's body tensed. "What kind of accident?"

"It's your parents, Alpha. They were in a car crash just outside the border. Your father… he only has minutes. You need to come. Now."
Ryker's blood ran cold. "Where are they?"

The pack member gave him an exact location, his tone growing more panicked. "Please, Alpha. Hurry."

Lara watched as Ryker hung up the phone, his face pale. "What's wrong?"

"It's my parents," Ryker said, his voice tight. "I need to go. They're barely holding on."

Rushing to Action

Ryker moved quickly, summoning several wolves to accompany him. Jessie offered to go, but Ryker shook his head.

"Stay here," Ryker ordered. "Keep an eye on Lara and Kael. If anything happens, call me immediately."
Jessie hesitated, his wolf growling softly in protest. "Are you sure?"

"I'm sure," Ryker said firmly. "I need you here."

Jessie nodded reluctantly, his gaze flicking to Lara. "I'll keep them safe."

Ryker turned to Lara, pulling her into a tight embrace. "I'll be back as soon as I can."

"Be careful," Lara whispered, her heart heavy with unease.

"I will," Ryker promised, pressing a kiss to her forehead.

A Morning Coffee

Shortly after Ryker left, the mansion fell quiet again. Jessie lingered nearby, pacing the hall outside Lara's room while the maids prepared breakfast.

Kate, Logan's girlfriend, appeared at the door with a tray of coffee, her face etched with worry. "Lara, I thought you might need this. It's been a rough morning."
Lara smiled faintly; her exhaustion evident. "Thank you, Kate. That's thoughtful."

Kate placed the tray on the small table near the window, her hands trembling slightly. "I still can't believe everything that's happening. Logan said the crash was horrible."

Lara frowned, her wolf stirring uneasily. "Logan knew about it?"

Kate hesitated, biting her lip. "He overheard someone talking. That's all."

Lara's suspicions flared, but she forced a smile. "I'm sure Ryker will handle it."

Kate nodded, stepping back as Lara reached for the coffee.

The Trap is Sprung

The moment Lara took a sip, she knew something was wrong. A strange bitterness lingered on her tongue, and her vision blurred almost immediately.
Her wolf growled in alarm, but its voice felt distant, muffled.

"Jessie…" Lara called weakly, her voice barely above a whisper. Her body swayed, and the coffee cup slipped from her hand, shattering on the floor.

Jessie burst into the room; his eyes wide with panic as he caught Lara before she collapsed. "Lara! What's happening?"

"I… don't know," she whispered, her words slurring.

Kate was at her side instantly, her face pale with fear. "What's wrong with her? Is she okay?" Jessie growled low, his wolf bristling. "Get the doctor. Now!" Kate nodded frantically, rushing from the room as the guards outside stepped in to assist Jessie.

The Distraction

As the guards and Jessie worked to tend to Lara, Logan moved quickly. He slipped into the nursery, his movements silent and deliberate.

Kael was sound asleep in his bassinet, his soft glow illuminating the room.

Logan hesitated for a brief moment, his hand hovering over the baby. His face twisted with something unreadable—fear, determination, perhaps even guilt—but he steeled himself and lifted Kael carefully into his arms.

The baby stirred but didn't cry, his tiny hand brushing against Logan's chest as though sensing something was wrong.

Logan glanced over his shoulder, listening for any sign of interruption. When he heard the commotion still coming from Lara's room, he slipped out the side door, disappearing into the forest before anyone noticed he was gone.

The Aftermath

It wasn't until several minutes later that Jessie realized something was wrong.

"Where's Kael?" he demanded, his voice sharp as he turned to the guards.

One of the maids gasped, her hand flying to her mouth. "He's in the nursery—"

Jessie didn't wait for her to finish. He sprinted down the hall, his wolf roaring inside him as he burst into the nursery. The empty bassinet confirmed his worst fears. "Damn it!" Jessie growled, slamming his fist against the wall.

He pulled out his phone, dialling Ryker with shaking hands. Ryker answered on the first ring; his voice filled with tension. "Jessie, what is it?"

"It's Kael," Jessie said, his voice shaking. "He's gone. Logan took him." Ryker's wolf roared through the bond, its fury crashing into Jessie like a tidal wave. "I'm on my way."

As the call ended, Ryker turned to his wolves, his face a mask of rage. "We've been played. Get back to the mansion. Now."

Back at the mansion, Lara stirred weakly, her wolf growling faintly in her mind. She forced her eyes open, her voice trembling as she whispered, "Where's Kael?"

Jessie knelt beside her, his face pale but determined. "We'll get him back, Lara. I swear."

Chapter 35: The Silence Before the Storm

The mansion felt hollow, as though it's very walls absorbed the grief and dread that had taken hold. The air was thick with tension, the kind that suffocates and leaves behind an ache too heavy to bear. Lara lay motionless in the master suite, her breaths soft but steady, her wolf silent for the first time since her shift at eighteen.

Ryker stood at her bedside, his hand gripping hers as if his sheer will alone pull her back. His eyes, usually so sharp and commanding, were clouded with fear. For the first time in years, the alpha felt powerless.

"Lara," he whispered, his voice cracking. "Please wake up."

Her face, so peaceful in sleep, gave no indication she had heard him. Her wolf, her constant companion, was dormant. There was no growl, no stirring presence in her mind. Just an eerie, unnatural quiet.

The Mansion in Chaos

Jessie paced the hallway outside the bedroom, his wolf growling incessantly. The guards avoided his gaze, knowing the beta was barely holding himself together. The tension was palpable, every second stretching longer than the last.

"I should have stopped him," Jessie growled under his breath, his fists clenching.

Maeve placed a hand on his shoulder, her calm presence doing little to soothe him. "This isn't your fault, Jessie. Logan planned this. He used Kate and her connection to Lara to get close. No one could have predicted this."

Jessie shook his head, his jaw tightening. “I should have been faster. Smarter.”

A Race Against Time

Ryker emerged from the room, his eyes like steel. The vulnerability he had shown by Lara’s side was gone, replaced by the alpha who led an unstoppable pack.

“We’re going after him,” Ryker said, his voice low and commanding. Jessie nodded immediately. “I’ve already organized patrols. We have wolves searching the perimeter.”

Ryker’s jaw tightened. “It’s not enough. I’m leading this hunt myself.” “What about Lara?” Jessie asked, hesitating.

Ryker’s gaze flickered briefly; the weight of his decision evident. “She’s stable. But I can’t stay here and wait while he has my son. I need to act.”

Maeve stepped forward; her tone soft but firm. “She needs you too, Ryker.” “I’ll bring him back,” Ryker said, his voice resolute. “Both of them.”

The Plan

The pack assembled in the forest clearing just beyond the mansion, their faces grim as Ryker outlined the plan. Jessie, Caleb, and Ben stood closest; their loyalty unwavering.

“We’ll split into three groups,” Ryker said, his voice carrying through the night air. “Logan can’t have gotten far. He’s on foot, and Kael is with him. He’ll be slowed down.”

“What about Kate?” Jessie asked, his brow furrowing. “She’s being held,” Ryker replied. “We’ll deal with her later. Right now, the priority is Kael.” Jessie growled low. “She’s just as guilty as Logan." Ryker's eyes flashed. "We don't know that yet. Focus on the hunt."

The Trail

The wolves shifted seamlessly, their forms powerful and sleek as they darted into the forest. Ryker led his group, his black wolf moving like a shadow through the trees. The scent of Kael clung faintly to the air, mingled with Logan's unfamiliar smell.

"He's heading east," Ryker said through the mind-link, his voice sharp and focused. "Don't lose him."

The trail was erratic, as though Logan had tried to confuse them. It wove through dense undergrowth, doubled back on itself, and crossed a shallow stream. But Ryker's wolf was relentless, his instincts homing in on the faint traces left behind.

An Unexpected Turn

Hours passed, and the trail grew colder. The wolves regrouped near the edge of a cliff overlooking a wide expanse of forest. The moonlight illuminated the treetops, casting eerie shadows that danced with the wind.

"We're losing time," Jessie said, shifting back into his human form. Ryker growled, his wolf pacing restlessly. "He's close. I can feel it."

It was then that Maeve arrived, her wolf breathless but her eyes sharp. "Alpha, there's something you need to see."

She led them to a clearing not far from the cliff's edge. In the centre, a small fire burned low, its embers glowing faintly. Scattered around it were items that made Ryker's blood run cold—a single baby blanket, a bottle of milk, and a small crescent moon pendant identical to the one Lara once wore.

"He's taunting us," Ryker growled, his voice a low rumble.

Jessie crouched near the fire, his brow furrowing. "Why leave these behind? He's smarter than this." Maeve's gaze shifted to the shadows beyond the clearing. "Because he wants us to follow."

A Trap Revealed

The wolves pressed forward cautiously, their instincts screaming that something was wrong. The air grew heavier, tinged with an unnatural chill that set their fur on edge.

Ryker's wolf halted suddenly, his ears twitching as he caught a faint sound—laughter, high and chilling, echoing through the trees.

"Show yourself!" Ryker growled through the mind-link, his voice booming. The laughter stopped abruptly, replaced by a low, mocking voice. "You're persistent, Alpha. I'll give you that."

Logan stepped into view; his face twisted with a smug smile. In his arms, Kael lay bundled tightly, his glow dim but steady. Ryker's wolf snarled; his body coiled to strike. "Let him go, Logan."

Logan chuckled, his grip on Kael tightening. "Do you even know what he is, Ryker? What you've created? This child isn't just an heir. He's something far more dangerous."
Ryker's growl deepened, his wolf on the verge of snapping. "You don't know what you're talking about."

"Oh, but I do," Logan said, his eyes gleaming with malice. "Do you think that crescent moon mark is a blessing? It's a curse. A beacon for power that will attract every vampire, rogue, and hunter for miles."

Jessie stepped forward; his voice sharp. "You're lying."

Logan sneered. "Am I? Ask yourself, Alpha—why did the crescent moon necklace pass to him? Why did Lara fall into that unnatural sleep? The boy is draining her. Taking everything, she has to fuel his own strength."

Ryker froze, his wolf growling low in his chest. "You're lying," he said, though doubt crept into his voice.

"Am I?" Logan repeated, his tone mocking.

The Suspense Peaks

Before Ryker could respond, Logan raised a hand, his eyes flashing with a dark energy that made the wolves falter. The ground beneath them trembled, a low rumble growing louder with each passing second.

"You thought you could outsmart me," Logan said, his voice rising. "But this has been in motion long before your precious heir was born. He's the key to everything. And I'm going to make sure he fulfils his destiny."

With a blinding flash of light, Logan vanished, taking Kael with him.

Ryker's wolf roared, his howl echoing through the forest as he lunged toward the spot where Logan had stood. But it was too late. The air was empty, and the trail was gone.

A New Mystery

Ryker shifted back, his chest heaving as rage and fear battled within him. Jessie placed a hand on his shoulder, his own face pale.

“What do we do now?” Jessie asked, his voice barely above a whisper.

Ryker’s grey eyes burned with determination as he stared into the darkness. “We find him. We end this.”

Back at the mansion, Lara remained motionless, her breaths shallow as the crescent moon mark on her son’s chest began to glow faintly in the distance, as though tethered to her very soul.

Chapter 36: The Glow of the Moon

The mansion was cloaked in a somber silence, the air heavy with tension and dread. The pack was shaken—its alpha heir was gone, stolen by a traitor, and its Luna lay motionless in her bed, her radiant glow a haunting reminder of her unusual state.

Though Lara's glow had intensified, her condition remained unchanged. Her breaths were steady, but her body was unresponsive, and even her wolf was silent. The room seemed charged, as though the moon itself was watching, waiting for something to break the stillness.

Lara's Glow

Maeve knelt by Lara's bedside, her hand hovering just above Lara's glowing skin. The light wasn't natural; it shimmered softly, casting an ethereal glow over the room. It was unlike anything Maeve had ever seen, a radiance that seemed to hum with ancient power.

"This isn't just a reaction to Kael," Maeve murmured, her voice filled with awe. "It's something more."

Ryker, pacing near the window, turned sharply. "What do you mean?" Maeve looked up at him, her expression grave. "The glow—it's not because she's drained. It's because she's fighting." "Fighting what?" Ryker demanded, his voice edged with desperation.

Maeve hesitated before speaking. "A poison. There's something in her system, something unnatural."
Ryker's body tensed, his wolf growling low in his chest. "The coffee," he said, his voice a dangerous whisper.

Maeve nodded. “It’s likely. Whatever was in it is keeping her in this state, but the glow… that’s not normal either. It’s protecting her, somehow.”

The Moon Goddess’ Presence

As Maeve spoke, the glow around Lara flickered faintly, pulsing in time with her heartbeat. A cool breeze drifted through the room, carrying with it a faint, otherworldly scent of jasmine and moonlight.

Maeve’s eyes widened, her voice trembling. “She’s being watched.”

Ryker stepped closer, his grey eyes narrowing. “Watched by who?”
“The Moon Goddess,” Maeve whispered, her voice reverent. “She’s protecting Lara. That glow isn’t just her strength—it’s divine intervention.”

Ryker’s heart tightened. He dropped to his knees beside Lara’s bed, his hand covering hers. “If she’s protecting her, why isn’t Lara waking up? Why isn’t she helping Kael?”

Maeve placed a hand on his shoulder, her expression soft but firm. “The Moon Goddess doesn’t intervene directly. She gives us the tools we need to fight our battles, but it’s up to us to use them.”

The Plan

Ryker stood, his resolve hardening. “Then we fight.”

He turned to Jessie, who had been leaning against the doorframe, his arms crossed and his face grim.

"We'll track Logan, and this time, we won't stop until we have Kael," Ryker said.

Jessie nodded, his wolf stirring restlessly. "I've already got patrols sweeping the territory. But if he's left the borders…"

Ryker growled low, his dominance filling the room. "He won't get far. He's carrying Kael. Even with whatever powers he's using, he's not faster than my pack."

Maeve stepped forward. "If he used poison, he's not just any rogue. He's connected to something bigger."

"Then we'll find out who," Ryker said.

Gathering Allies

Ryker summoned the pack's top warriors to the war room, a space deep within the mansion that was lined with maps and communication devices. The wolves gathered quickly, their faces set with determination as Ryker laid out the plan.

"Logan isn't acting alone," Ryker began, his voice steady but cold. "Someone wanted my son, and they used him to do it. We're going to track him, but we're not just looking for him—we're looking for the bigger threat."

Jessie stepped forward, pointing to a map spread across the table. "The last trace of his scent was here, near the eastern ridge. If he's smart, he'll be heading for the human towns to mask his trail."

Ryker nodded. "I want patrols on every route out of the territory. Jessie, you'll lead the northern group. Caleb, take the west. I'll go east."

"What about the south?" Maeve asked.

Ryker's eyes darkened. "The south leads to vampire territory. If he goes that way, we'll know exactly who's pulling the strings."

The Chase

As the wolves set out, the forest grew eerily quiet, the usual hum of life silenced as though the world itself held its breath. Ryker led his group eastward, his black wolf moving swiftly through the underbrush.

The trail was faint but present, a mixture of Kael's soft glow and Logan's sharp, unfamiliar scent.

"He's fast," Ryker growled through the mind-link. "But he can't keep this up forever."

A Twisted Discovery

Hours into the chase, Ryker's group stumbled upon a strange sight—a small clearing littered with symbols carved into the ground. The markings glowed faintly, pulsing with a dark, unnatural energy.

Ryker shifted back, his chest heaving as he inspected the symbols. Jessie joined him, his eyes narrowing.

"What the hell is this?" Jessie muttered.

Maeve, who had followed them, knelt by the markings, her expression grim. "These are runes. Dark magic."
Ryker growled, his wolf bristling. "Logan isn't just working for someone. He's using magic to cover his tracks."

Maeve nodded; her voice steady. "He's masking Kael's scent. It's why the trail keeps going cold."

A Vision of Hope

As they regrouped, a soft, ethereal light appeared in the clearing. It wasn't the harsh glow of the runes but a soft, silver light that bathed the wolves in warmth.

The pack froze, their wolves growling softly as a figure began to take shape within the light.

"The Moon Goddess," Maeve whispered, her voice trembling.

The figure didn't speak, but its presence was overwhelming. The light washed over Ryker, and in that moment, he felt a surge of strength and clarity unlike anything he'd ever known.

When the light faded, the runes were gone, and the faint trace of Kael's scent returned.

"She's guiding us," Ryker said, his voice filled with quiet awe.

The pack pressed forward; their resolve strengthened. But as they neared the edge of their territory, a sudden, chilling howl echoed through the trees.

Ryker froze, his wolf growling low. The howl wasn't one of his wolves. It was something else—something darker.

Jessie stepped closer, his voice tense. "That's not Logan."

Ryker's eyes narrowed. "No. It's something worse."

The forest seemed to hold its breath as the howl echoed again, louder and closer. Ryker's wolf bristled, its growl rising in his chest.

"We keep moving," Ryker said, his voice a low rumble. "No matter what's out there, we're getting my son back."

As the pack moved forward, the suspense thickened, each step bringing them closer to the unknown. The faint glow of Kael's presence pulsed faintly in the distance, a beacon of hope against the darkness closing in.

Chapter 37: The Predator in the Shadows

The forest had never felt so oppressive. The ancient trees, usually a source of comfort and grounding for the pack, seemed to loom taller, their branches twisting unnaturally in the soft moonlight. The scent of Kael was faint but present, a whisper of hope that kept Ryker and his wolves pushing forward. But with every step, the air grew colder, heavier, as though something was watching them from the shadows.

Ryker's black wolf led the way, his massive paws silent against the soft earth. His muscles coiled with tension, his ears twitching at every faint rustle. He could feel it—a presence trailing them, keeping its distance but never truly leaving.

Behind him, Jessie and the other wolves followed closely, their movements cautious but ready for a fight. The bond through their mind-link was taut, a shared unease that none of them could shake.

"Whatever this is, it's not Logan," Jessie said through the link, his voice low and wary.

"No," Ryker growled in reply, his wolf bristling. "It's something else."

The Trail Grows Cold

They reached a small clearing, the moonlight casting eerie patterns across the ground. The scent of Kael disappeared abruptly, as though swallowed by the cold, still air.

Ryker shifted back into his human form, his chest heaving as he scanned the area.

"This doesn't make sense," Jessie muttered, shifting as well. He crouched near the ground, his fingers brushing over the dirt. "It's like the trail just… stopped."

Ryker's jaw tightened, his eyes narrowing. "It's not natural. Logan's using magic again to cover his tracks."
Maeve stepped forward, her eyes scanning the perimeter. "It's more than that. This area—it's wrong."

Ryker turned to her, his voice sharp. "What do you mean?"

Maeve gestured to the trees, their twisted branches forming unnatural shapes. "The energy here. It's not just dark—it's alive."

As if to confirm her words, a low, guttural growl echoed from the forest, sending a chill down everyone's spine.

The First Encounter

The pack froze, their wolves bristling as the growl grew louder, closer. It wasn't the sound of a rogue or even a wild animal. It was deeper, more guttural, like the earth itself was growling.

Ryker stepped forward, his grey eyes scanning the shadows. "Show yourself," he commanded, his voice a low rumble.

For a moment, there was silence. Then, from the darkness, a pair of glowing red eyes emerged, their gaze fixed on Ryker.

The creature stepped into the moonlight, and a collective gasp rippled through the pack. It was unlike anything they had seen before—a monstrous hybrid of wolf and shadow, its body shifting and flickering like smoke. Its claws were long and sharp, its teeth bared in a snarl that seemed to vibrate through the air.

"What in the hell is that?" Jessie growled, his wolf bristling.

"A shadow wolf," Maeve whispered, her voice trembling.

Ryker's eyes narrowed. "They're extinct."

"Not anymore," Maeve replied, her face pale. "And they're hunters. If it's here, it's not by chance."

The First Strike

The shadow wolf lunged without warning; its speed almost too fast to follow. Ryker shifted mid-air, his black wolf colliding with the creature in a clash of fur and claws. The impact sent shockwaves through the clearing, the sound of snarls and growls tearing through the night.

The pack moved to assist, but Ryker growled through the mind-link. "Stay back. This is mine."

Jessie hesitated, his wolf pacing anxiously, but he obeyed. Ryker's dominance was undeniable, and this fight was his alone.

The shadow wolf was unlike any opponent Ryker had faced. Its body moved with unnatural fluidity, twisting and shifting as though it were made of smoke. Each strike he landed seemed to dissipate into nothingness, the creature reforming instantly.

“You can’t kill it like this,” Maeve said through the link, her voice urgent. “Shadow wolves are immune to physical attacks. You need magic—or fire.”

A Tactical Retreat

Realizing he couldn’t defeat the creature without preparation, Ryker shifted back, his chest heaving. “We need to regroup,” he said aloud, his voice firm.

The shadow wolf growled low, its red eyes burning as it advanced. Ryker stood his ground, his wolf snarling in his mind.

“Jessie, get the others back to the mansion,” Ryker ordered. “Maeve, come with me. We need answers.”
Jessie hesitated, his loyalty warring with his instincts. “What about you?”

“I’ll be fine,” Ryker said, his tone leaving no room for argument. “Go.”

Reluctantly, Jessie led the others back toward the mansion, leaving Ryker and Maeve alone in the clearing.

A Deeper Mystery

The shadow wolf didn’t attack immediately. It circled Ryker and Maeve, its red eyes gleaming with something almost intelligent.
“It’s waiting,” Maeve said softly, her voice tense.

“For what?” Ryker asked, his dark eyes locked on the creature. Maeve hesitated. “For us to make a mistake.”

Ryker growled low, his wolf pacing restlessly. “We need to draw it out. If it’s waiting for us, it’s because it knows we’re a threat.” Maeve nodded, her hands glowing faintly as she summoned a protective barrier. “I’ll hold it off. You figure out how to stop it.”

A Battle of Wits

The shadow wolf lunged again, its movements a blur. Maeve’s barrier held, the creature’s claws scraping against the glowing shield with a sound that made Ryker’s teeth ache.

“Whatever magic it’s using, it’s strong,” Maeve said, sweat beading on her forehead. “This isn’t just a rogue summoning. This is ancient.”

Ryker’s mind raced. If the shadow wolf was connected to Logan, it meant this wasn’t just about Kael—it was about power.

“Can you weaken it?” Ryker asked, his voice sharp. “I can try,” Maeve said, her hands glowing brighter.

The Turning Point

As Maeve chanted softly, the shadow wolf hesitated, its movements slowing. Ryker saw his opening and shifted, his black wolf lunging forward with a ferocity that sent the creature reeling.
But just as Ryker landed a blow, the shadow wolf dissolved into smoke, disappearing into the night.

"What the hell?" Ryker growled, shifting back. "It's not gone," Maeve said, her voice trembling. "It's retreating. But it'll be back."

A Revelation

As the forest fell silent, Maeve turned to Ryker, her face pale.

"This wasn't just an attack," she said. "This was a warning. Logan didn't summon the shadow wolf—it's hunting him too. And if that's true…"

Ryker's eyes narrowed. "What?" Maeve hesitated before speaking. "Then Kael isn't just a target. He's the key to controlling it." The weight of her words settled over them like a storm, and Ryker's wolf growled low in his chest.

"We need to move fast," Ryker said, his voice steady but cold. "Because if they get to Kael before we do, it won't just be him in danger. It'll be all of us."

Chapter 38: The Calm Before the Storm

The forest seemed darker than usual, as though the moon was withholding its light in preparation for something far greater. A faint mist curled between the trees, and the distant sounds of nocturnal creatures only emphasized the unnatural silence hanging over the clearing. Ryker stood at the edge of a cliff, his sharp dark eyes scanning the vast expanse of wilderness below. He could feel the full moon's energy pulling at his wolf, promising strength and clarity when the time came. But the storm brewing within him would not wait for the moon's peak.

He clenched his fists, his jaw tight as he thought of Kael—his son, his heir—stolen and in the hands of someone who would do anything to harness his power. The anger coiling within Ryker was tempered only by the sharp focus of his mind as he pieced together every fragment of information they had gathered.

A Night to Plan

Back at the campsite near the edge of the territory, the remaining wolves worked quickly to prepare for what would come. A large map spread out over a makeshift table in the centre of the clearing was covered in marks and notes, evidence of hours spent retracing Logan's movements. Jessie stood to one side, his arms crossed as he watched Maeve and Caleb finalize patrol routes.

Ryker arrived; his steps purposeful as he joined the group. His black wolf had been restless all day, pacing in the back of his mind, growling with impatience.

"We need to assume Logan won't stop until he reaches his destination," Ryker began, his voice sharp and commanding. "And whatever's hunting him is going to keep coming after

us." Jessie nodded. "If Logan's using Kael for a ritual, it means he has a specific location in mind. Somewhere with power."

Maeve tapped a spot on the map. “There’s an old ruin here, just outside the southern border. It’s been abandoned for centuries, but if he’s working with dark magic, it’s the perfect place.”

Ryker’s gaze narrowed, his wolf growling softly. “Then that’s where we’ll go.” “What about the shadow wolf?” Caleb asked, his voice tense. “We can’t fight it with brute strength.”

Maeve nodded. “I’ve been researching shadow wolves since the attack. They’re tied to magic—ancient, destructive magic. But they’re not invincible. Fire disrupts their form, and light weakens them.”

“Light?” Jessie repeated, frowning.

“Specifically, moonlight,” Maeve clarified. “During a full moon, they’re at their weakest. If we can trap it in the moonlight and burn it with enchanted fire, we have a chance.”

Preparing the Pack

The decision was made to split into two groups. Ryker, Maeve, and a small team of elite fighters would leave immediately, heading south to intercept Logan before he could reach the ruins. Jessie, Caleb, and the remaining wolves would return to the mansion to inform the pack and rally reinforcements.

Before departing, Ryker addressed the group, his voice steady but filled with intensity.
“We have one night before the full moon,” he said, his gray eyes scanning their faces. “One night to stop Logan, protect my son, and destroy whatever threat this shadow wolf poses to our pack. We fight with everything we have. For Kael. For Lara. For the future of our pack.”

The wolves howled in unison, their voices echoing through the forest as Ryker shifted into his massive black wolf and led his group south.

Back at the Mansion

The mansion was a flurry of activity as Jessie and the others returned their urgency sparking immediate action. Guards were doubled, patrols expanded, and preparations for war began in earnest.

In the master suite, Lara lay motionless, her glow brightening with each passing hour. The pack doctor, Dr. Elden, worked tirelessly alongside Maeve to identify the poison that had been used. Lara's mother and father arrived shortly after; their faces etched with worry as they rushed to her side.

Her mother's voice trembled as she stroked Lara's hair. "She looks so peaceful, but it's not right. She should be awake."

"She's not just fighting," Dr. Elden said, his tone filled with awe. "She's healing. And growing stronger."

"What do you mean?" Lara's father asked, his voice tight.

Dr. Elden hesitated before answering. "Lara's a white wolf—an alpha unlike any other. Her body isn't just resisting the poison; it's adapting. Whatever was meant to harm her is being turned into strength."

Narrowing Down the Poison

The room fell silent as Dr. Elden and Maeve worked together, poring over ancient texts and records to identify the poison. After hours of research, Maeve finally spoke.
"It's not just a poison," she said, her voice grim. "It's a cursed brew—crafted to bind the soul and suppress the wolf."

"But why hasn't it killed her?" Lara's mother asked, her eyes wide.

"Because she's stronger than the curse," Maeve replied. "Her wolf is too powerful to suppress completely. The glow we're seeing is her soul fighting back."

Dr. Elden nodded. "She'll wake, but it will take time. And when she does, she won't be the same. She'll be stronger."

Ryker's Discovery

Meanwhile, Ryker and his team pushed deeper into the southern forest. As they neared the ruins, the air grew colder, carrying a faint metallic scent that made his wolf growl.

The ruins were shrouded in mist; their crumbling walls etched with ancient symbols that glowed faintly in the moonlight. In the centre of the clearing stood a stone altar, its surface slick with what appeared to be fresh blood.

Maeve gasped, her hand flying to her mouth. "This isn't just any ritual. This is sacrificial magic."

Ryker's wolf snarled, his rage building as he stepped closer to the altar. "What are they trying to do?"

Maeve's voice trembled as she answered. "If they're using Kael, it's to channel his purity. A white wolf's child is powerful, but

Kael is more than that. He's marked by the Moon Goddess. They're planning to use his essence to complete a spell that can only be performed once in a lifetime—a spell to summon true darkness."

Ryker's fists clenched, his body trembling with fury. "Over my dead body."

The Shadow Wolf Returns

Before Ryker could say more, a chilling howl tore through the ruins, and the shadow wolf emerged from the mist, its red eyes gleaming with malice.

The pack formed a defensive circle, their growls filling the air as the creature advanced.

"Maeve, light the fire," Ryker ordered, his voice sharp.

Maeve nodded; her hands glowing as she began to chant. The flames that erupted were bright and fierce, casting the ruins in an otherworldly light.

The shadow wolf snarled, its form flickering as the fire approached. But it didn't retreat. Instead, it lunged, its massive body colliding with Ryker's black wolf in a blur of claws and teeth.

The Battle Rages

The fight was brutal, the shadow wolf's claws tearing through flesh as Ryker fought with a ferocity unmatched by any wolf. The pack supported him, their combined efforts driving the creature back toward the altar.

Maeve's chants grew louder, the fire spreading until it surrounded the shadow wolf, trapping it in a circle of light.

"It's weakening!" Maeve shouted; her voice filled with urgency.

Ryker seized the opportunity, his wolf striking with lethal precision. The shadow wolf howled, its form flickering violently as the enchanted flames consumed it.

The Final Revelation

As the creature dissolved into smoke, a single word echoed through the ruins, spoken in a voice that seemed to come from everywhere and nowhere.

"Kael."

Ryker shifted back, his chest heaving as he stared at the altar. "This isn't over," he growled. "They still have him."

Maeve placed a hand on his arm, her expression grim. "But we've weakened their forces. And the full moon is on our side."

Ryker's eyes burned with determination as he turned to his pack. "We finish this. We bring him home."

Chapter 39: A Storm Unleashed

The southern ruins loomed before Ryker like the jagged teeth of a beast; their crumbling walls shrouded in mist and shadow. The scent of Kael was stronger here, mingling with the metallic tang of blood and the sickly-sweet stench of dark magic. Every fibre of Ryker's being vibrated with fury, his wolf growling deep in his chest as he stalked forward.

Behind him, Maeve and the elite fighters followed in tense silence, their eyes darting between the dark corners of the ruins. The air was heavy, almost suffocating, and the faint sound of chanting drifted through the mist.

Ryker's hands clenched into fists, his nails digging into his palms as he growled, "This ends now."

The Approach

The ruins were a labyrinth of broken stone and twisted paths. The once-grand archways now stood as jagged sentinels, their carvings worn and almost unrecognizable. Ryker moved with purpose, his sharp eyes scanning every shadow. The glow of the moon above illuminated his powerful frame, casting a menacing silhouette as he advanced.

Maeve whispered behind him; her voice barely audible. "The ritual is reaching its peak. We don't have much time."

Ryker didn't respond. His focus was singular, his fury bubbling dangerously close to the surface. His wolf snarled in his mind, demanding blood, demanding vengeance.

"They took my son."

The thought burned in his chest, fuelling the storm of dominance that radiated off him in waves.

The Enemy Revealed

As they rounded a crumbled wall, the ritual site came into view. In the centre of the ruins stood a large stone altar, its surface slick with fresh blood. Candles surrounded it in a precise pattern, their flames flickering unnaturally in the still air.

Logan stood at the altar; his face twisted with concentration as he chanted in a language that sounded ancient and guttural. His hands hovered over Kael, who lay on the altar wrapped in the same blue blanket Lara had held him in.

Kael was silent, his faint glow dimmed, but his small chest rose and fell with steady breaths.

Around the altar, a group of cloaked figures formed a circle, their faces obscured by shadows. They moved in unison, their hands raised as they chanted along with Logan.

The sight of his son on that cold, blood-streaked stone sent Ryker over the edge.

Ryker's Fury Unleashed

A deafening snarl tore from Ryker's throat as he charged forward, his black wolf erupting from within him in a blur of power and rage.

Logan's head snapped up, his chanting faltering as he stumbled back. "Stop him!" he shouted, his voice panicked.
The cloaked figures moved to intercept, but they were no match for Ryker. He tore through them with lethal precision, his claws raking across their chests and his jaws snapping at their throats. Each strike was calculated, driven by pure dominance and the unrelenting need to protect his son.

Maeve and the others joined the fight, their wolves darting through the chaos to take down the remaining figures. The air was filled with snarls, screams, and the sharp tang of blood as the battle raged on.

Logan's Desperation

Logan scrambled back, his hands shaking as he tried to summon another spell. "You don't understand what's at stake!" he shouted, his voice cracking.

Ryker shifted back into his human form, his chest heaving as he advanced on Logan. His grey eyes burned with a fury that made Logan falter.

"I don't care what you think you're doing," Ryker growled, his voice low and dangerous. "You took my son. That's the only thing that matters."

Logan raised his hands defensively, his lips curling into a desperate smile. "He's not just your son, Ryker. He's the key to something bigger—something you can't even begin to comprehend."

Ryker's fist connected with Logan's jaw, the force of the blow sending him crashing into the altar. "The only thing I comprehend," Ryker said, his voice like a growl, "is that you're a dead man."

The Fight Intensifies

Logan wiped the blood from his mouth, his face twisting with rage. "You think you've already won?" he spat. "You have no idea what's coming."

Before Ryker could respond, the ground beneath them trembled. Dark energy erupted from the altar, sending shockwaves through the ruins. The remaining cloaked figures dissolved into smoke, their forms merging with the swirling shadows that surrounded Logan.

The shadow wolf appeared again; its red eyes gleaming as it stepped out from the darkness. It growled low, its massive body rippling with power as it moved to stand beside Logan.
Ryker's wolf snarled, its growl echoing through the ruins as it prepared to strike.

Kael's Cry

As the battle raged on, a sound cut through the chaos—a high-pitched, desperate cry that made Ryker's heart lurch.
The baby's wail was sharp and filled with distress, his glow flickering as the dark energy around him intensified.

"Kael!" Ryker roared, his voice breaking as he turned toward the altar.

The sight of his son screaming on that cold, cursed stone made something snap within Ryker. His wolf surged forward, its dominance radiating so strongly that even the shadow wolf hesitated. "Get away from him!" Ryker's growl tore through the mind-link, his voice shaking the air.

Lara Awakens

Back at the mansion, the glow around Lara grew blinding, filling the room with an intense silver light that made everyone shield their eyes.

Dr. Elden stumbled back; his voice filled with awe. "She's waking up." Lara's mother clutched her hand tightly, her voice trembling. "Lara, can you hear me?"

Kael's distant scream echoed through the bond, faint but undeniable. Lara's fingers twitched, her breath hitching as her wolf stirred for the first time in days.

Inside her mind, the silence broke. "It's time," her wolf growled, its voice steady and strong. Lara's eyes snapped open, their usual blue now glowing with an otherworldly light.
Ryker stood at the altar; his body coiled to strike as Kael's cries grew louder. The shadow wolf lunged, its massive form aiming straight for Ryker.

But before it could reach him, a blinding silver light erupted from the distance, illuminating the ruins with the force of the moon itself. Ryker froze, his wolf growling low as the light washed over him. "Lara," he whispered, his voice filled with a mix of relief and awe.

The shadow wolf howled in pain, its form flickering as the light consumed it. Logan stumbled back, his face twisting in horror. "What is this?" he screamed, shielding his eyes.

The light grew stronger, more radiant, as Lara's presence filled the bond, her voice calm but commanding. "I'm coming."

Chapter 40: The Awakening of the White Wolf

The air around the ruins vibrated with tension as Logan's spell reached its climax. The dark energy swirling around the altar grew thicker, pulsing with an unnatural rhythm that seemed to echo through the forest. Kael's cries rose in desperation, piercing through the oppressive hum of magic.

Ryker stood his ground, his black wolf snarling in his mind, its growls mingling with the chorus of his elite warriors who flanked him. His gray eyes burned with fury as he glared at Logan, who now stood protected by the shadow wolf, its red eyes gleaming with malevolence.

"I'll give you one chance to hand over my son," Ryker growled, his voice cold and edged with lethal promise.

Logan's lips twisted into a sneer. "You're not in a position to demand anything, Alpha. The ritual is nearly complete. Kael's essence will fuel the greatest spell this world has ever known. Your fight is meaningless."

Ryker's wolf roared in his mind, its rage building as the scent of Kael's distress filled the air. "We'll see about that," Ryker snarled, stepping forward, his dominance radiating like a physical force.

The shadow wolf moved to intercept him, its massive body rippling as it lunged. But before it could reach Ryker, the ruins were flooded with a sudden, blinding light.

Lara's Arrival

The light was pure and silvery, cutting through the darkness like the first rays of dawn after a storm. It washed over the ruins, illuminating every corner and casting sharp shadows against the

crumbling walls. The oppressive hum of dark magic faltered, the swirling energy around the altar thinning as though repelled by the light.

Logan stumbled back, his expression twisting into one of disbelief. "No… it can't be."

The shadow wolf howled, its form flickering and weakening as the light grew stronger.

Ryker turned toward the source of the light, his breath catching in his chest. Standing at the edge of the ruins was Lara.

Her hair, usually a soft cascade of gold, now shimmered with silver streaks that seemed to glow in the moonlight. Her eyes blazed with a radiant blue fire; their intensity almost otherworldly. The air around her shimmered, a faint aura of power rippling outward like heatwaves.

Her wolf, fully awake and fully present, radiated dominance and purity, its growl a low, constant rumble in her mind. "We are the White Wolf," it growled. "And we are done waiting."

The Moment of Power

Lara stepped forward, her movements fluid and purposeful. Each step seemed to shake the ground, the ancient stones of the ruins resonating with her power. The glow around her intensified, pulsing in time with her heartbeat, and the pack wolves instinctively bowed their heads, their wolves submitting to her without hesitation.

Ryker's heart swelled with pride and relief as he met her gaze. Through their bond, he felt her strength, her love, and her unyielding determination.

"You came," he said through the mind-link, his voice a mixture of awe and gratitude. "I'll always come," Lara replied, her voice steady but filled with emotion.

Logan's voice broke through the moment, his tone frantic and disbelieving. "This isn't possible! The poison should have kept you down!"
Lara turned her gaze to him, her expression cold and unyielding. "You underestimated me. You underestimated my family."

The Rescue

Kael's cries grew louder as Lara approached the altar. The dark magic surrounding it lashed out like tendrils, trying to keep her at bay. But the light radiating from her form burned away the darkness, each step she took dissolving the corrupted energy.

Logan shouted an incantation, his voice desperate as he tried to reinforce the spell. The shadow wolf lunged again, its body flickering with renewed strength.

Ryker intercepted it, his black wolf meeting the creature mid-air in a clash of teeth and claws. The force of their collision sent shockwaves through the ruins, but Ryker's strength was unmatched. He slammed the shadow wolf into the ground, his dominance overwhelming as he tore into it with a ferocity that left no room for escape.

Lara reached the altar, her hands trembling as she gently lifted Kael from its bloodied surface. The moment their skin touched, the glow around her pulsed brighter, and Kael's cries softened into quiet coos.

"It's okay, my love," Lara whispered, holding him close. "Mama's here."

The Full Awakening

As Lara cradled Kael, the glow around her intensified, expanding outward in a radiant burst of light. The ruins trembled as the energy washed over them, the dark magic dissolving like smoke in the wind.

Logan screamed, his body recoiling as the light seared through him. "No! This isn't how it's supposed to end!"

Lara turned her gaze to him, her voice steady and commanding. "You made a mistake when you came for my family. Now you'll face the consequences."

The light around her began to shift, forming tendrils of energy that snaked toward Logan and the remnants of the shadow wolf. The tendrils wrapped around them, holding them in place as Lara's power surged.

"This ends here," she said, her voice echoing with an almost divine authority.

Ryker's Role

Ryker shifted back into his human form, his chest heaving as he stood beside Lara. His eyes blazed with pride and determination as he placed a hand on her shoulder.

"We do this together," he said, his voice low but firm.

Lara nodded, her gaze softening as she looked at him. "Always."

The light around them pulsed again, and together, they unleashed their combined strength. The ruins shook violently as the energy exploded outward, obliterating the shadow wolf and severing the last remnants of Logan's spell.

When the dust settled, Logan lay on the ground, his body battered, and his aura of power completely gone.

Kael cooed softly in Lara's arms, his glow now bright and steady as he snuggled against her chest. The ruins were silent, the oppressive energy replaced by a calm stillness.

But as Ryker and Lara turned to leave, a faint, chilling voice echoed through the ruins.

"This isn't over," it said, the words barely more than a whisper but carrying a promise of darkness.

Ryker's wolf growled, his protective instincts flaring as he placed a hand on Lara's back. "We'll be ready," he said, his voice steady but edged with rage.

Lara tightened her hold on Kael, her glowing eyes narrowing as she replied, "Let them come."

Chapter 41: Strength in Unity

The aftermath of the battle left the pack shaken but victorious. The southern ruins were quiet now, stripped of their dark energy, and the moon's light cascaded over the broken stone in soft, calming waves. Ryker and Lara stood at the centre of it all, their son cradled between them.

Kael cooed softly, his glow steady and warm, as though the power within him had stabilized. His tiny fingers wrapped around Lara's thumb, anchoring her to the moment after so much chaos.

Ryker's arm rested protectively around Lara's waist, his gray eyes scanning the horizon for any lingering threats. But for the first time in what felt like days, the tension in his shoulders began to ease.

"He's safe," Ryker said, his voice low and soothing.

Lara nodded, brushing a soft kiss against Kael's forehead. "We're safe."

Her wolf purred softly in agreement, its presence stronger and more confident than ever.

The Return to the Mansion

By the time they returned to the mansion, the first hints of dawn were painting the sky in soft hues of pink and gold. The pack was waiting for them, their cheers and howls filling the air as Ryker and Lara stepped through the gates with Kael in their arms.

Jessie was the first to approach, his face breaking into a wide grin. "You did it," he said, clapping Ryker on the shoulder.

"We did it," Ryker corrected, his voice filled with gratitude.

Maeve stepped forward, her expression a mixture of awe and relief as she bowed her head to Lara. “Luna,” she said softly. “Your strength is… beyond anything I’ve ever seen.” Lara smiled faintly, exhaustion tugging at her features. “Thank you, Maeve. For everything.”

A Moment Alone

Later that evening, after Kael was settled in his bassinet and the mansion had quieted, Ryker found Lara standing by the window of their bedroom. The moonlight bathed her in silver, highlighting the soft glow that still lingered around her.

He stepped up behind her, his hands settling on her hips as he pressed his chest against her back.

“You were incredible today,” Ryker murmured, his lips brushing against her ear. Lara leaned into him, her body relaxing under his touch. “So were you.”

Ryker’s grip tightened slightly, his wolf growling softly in the back of his mind. “You scared me,” he admitted, his voice rough with emotion. “When you were asleep… I didn’t know if I’d ever see you wake up.”

Lara turned in his arms, her blue eyes locking onto his. “I’m here,” she said softly, her hand resting against his cheek. “And I always will be.”

A Sensual Reunion

Ryker’s eyes darkened, his wolf growling louder as he leaned down, capturing her lips in a kiss that was slow and consuming. His hands slid up her sides, pulling her closer as the tension of the past days melted away into something deeper.

Lara's fingers tangled in his hair, a soft moan escaping her lips as she pressed against him. Her wolf purred in the back of her mind; its approval clear as Ryker's dominance washed over her in waves.

"You're mine," Ryker growled against her lips, his voice thick with desire.

"And you're mine," Lara replied, her voice breathless but steady.

Ryker lifted her effortlessly, carrying her to the bed as his lips trailed along her jaw and down her neck. He laid her down gently, his body hovering over hers as he took a moment to drink her in.

"You're perfect," he murmured, his grey eyes filled with adoration and heat.

Lara's cheeks flushed as she reached up, pulling him down into another kiss. Their movements were slow and deliberate, each touch and kiss a reminder of their bond and the strength they drew from one another.

Ryker's hands explored her body with reverence, his lips following the path of his fingers as he worshipped her. Lara responded with equal fervour, her nails dragging lightly down his back, eliciting a low growl from deep in his chest.

The room was filled with the sounds of their shared passion, the outside world forgotten as they lost themselves in each other. She felt the press of his body against hers—warm, insistent—and every nerve ending in her skin sang with the promise of more.

His breath fluttered over her collarbone, light as moth wings, and she arched into the delicious tension he wove between them. She surrendered to the soft thud of his heartbeat against her chest, matching her own as she tilted her head back for his mouth.

His lips ghosted from her shoulder to the curve of her neck, and she trembled at each feather-light kiss. She threaded her fingers through the fabric of his shirt, pulling him deeper into that intoxicating orbit he'd created around her. Every drag of his fingertips along her ribs felt like an electric current, leaving her quivering in its wake. She caught the soft gasp he drew when her hand found the edge of his waistband—both an invitation and a confession.

His mouth claimed hers in a kiss that consumed her senses, world and time collapsing until there was only heat and breath and skin. She clung to him as if letting go would unravel her, every curve and hollow of her body memorized by the hushed urgency of his touch.

The Morning After

The first rays of sunlight streamed through the curtains, casting a warm glow over the room. Lara stirred; her body comfortably tangled with Ryker's as they lay entwined in the aftermath of their night together.

Ryker woke moments later, his arm tightening around her as he nuzzled into her neck. "Good morning, love," he murmured, his voice still thick with sleep.

Lara smiled, her fingers tracing lazy patterns on his chest. "Good morning." They lay in silence for a while, savouring the peaceful moment. But soon, the sounds of the pack stirring reminded them of the responsibilities waiting outside their door.

"We should get up," Lara said softly, though she made no move to leave the warmth of his embrace.

"Not yet," Ryker replied, his lips brushing against her forehead. "Just a little longer."

A Celebration Feast

By evening, the pack gathered in the great hall to celebrate their victory and the safe return of their alpha heir. The room was adorned with flowers and glowing lanterns, their light casting a warm and inviting glow over the long banquet tables laden with food.

Laughter and music filled the air as pack members shared stories and toasted to the future.

Lara and Ryker sat at the head table; Kael nestled in Lara's arms as he cooed softly. The pack's love and admiration for their alphas were palpable, their howls of celebration echoing through the night.

Jessie stood to make a toast, his voice carrying over the din. "To Ryker and Lara," he said, raising his glass. "Our leaders, our protectors, and the strongest wolves I've ever known. And to Kael, the future of our pack."

The room erupted in cheers, the sound filling every corner of the mansion as Ryker and Lara exchanged a smile.

In that moment, surrounded by their pack and their family, they knew they had everything they needed to face whatever came next.

Chapter 42: Strengthened by Love

Time passed with a steady rhythm at the mansion, but for Ryker and Lara, the days blurred into moments of joy, passion, and quiet strength. Kael's presence brought a new energy to their lives, his bright glow a constant reminder of the bond they had forged through trials and triumphs.

The pack was thriving under their leadership. The balance they had fought so hard to maintain was stronger than ever, but with stability came the space to reflect, grow, and rediscover the intimacy that made Ryker and Lara unstoppable.

A Quiet Morning Together

It was early, the sky painted with the soft hues of dawn, when Lara stirred in their bed. Ryker's arm was draped over her waist, his breathing deep and even as he slept beside her. She shifted slightly, her hand resting on his chest, feeling the steady thrum of his heartbeat.

Her wolf purred in her mind, content and sated. "This is our mate. Our home. Our everything."

Ryker stirred, his grey eyes blinking open as a slow, lazy smile spread across his face. "You're awake," he murmured, his voice husky with sleep.

"So are you," Lara teased, her fingers tracing idle patterns on his chest.

Ryker growled softly, rolling onto his side to face her fully. "How could I not be, with you beside me?"

Lara laughed, the sound light and carefree. "Flatterer."
"It's not flattery if it's true," Ryker replied, his hand sliding to her hip as he pulled her closer.

Deepening the Connection

The soft morning light streamed through the curtains, casting a warm glow over the room as Ryker pressed a kiss to Lara's temple.

"You've changed everything," he said quietly, his voice filled with reverence. "The pack. My life. I didn't know it was possible to feel this much love."

Lara looked up at him, her blue eyes shining. "You've given me everything I've ever wanted, Ryker. Love, family, a home."

Ryker's gaze darkened, his wolf growling softly as he leaned down, his lips brushing against hers in a kiss that was slow and consuming. "You're mine," he murmured against her lips, his voice low and possessive.

"And you're mine," Lara whispered, her hands tangling in his hair as she deepened the kiss.

Their movements were deliberate, filled with the kind of passion that only came from true understanding and devotion. Ryker's touch was firm but tender, his dominance tempered by the deep respect and love he felt for her.

Kael's Growth

As the months passed, Kael grew stronger and brighter, his unique glow captivating everyone who saw him. From the moment he took his first steps, it was clear that Kael was no ordinary pup. His wolf stirred early, its presence evident in his piercing blue eyes and the strength of his small frame.

"He's going to be incredible," Jessie said one day as he watched Kael toddle across the great hall, his laughter echoing off the walls.

Ryker, standing nearby, nodded with pride. “He already is.”

Kael’s abilities began to manifest in small but extraordinary ways. He could sense emotions with uncanny accuracy, his presence calming even the most agitated pack members. And when he played with the other pups, there was an undeniable energy about him—a natural leadership that drew others to him.

“He’s going to be a great alpha one day,” Lara said softly one evening as she watched Kael sleep, his tiny hand clutching the edge of his blanket.

Ryker wrapped an arm around her shoulders, his voice steady. “With you as his mother, there’s no doubt about it.”

Challenges and Legacy

As Kael grew, so did the responsibility of preparing him for the future. Lara and Ryker worked together to ensure he understood the importance of his role—not just as their son, but as the heir to a legacy that spanned generations.

One evening, Ryker and Lara took Kael to the ceremonial grounds deep within the forest, where the pack had gathered to honour their history.

“Kael,” Ryker said, kneeling in front of his son. “This is where your ancestors stood. This is where they made the choices that shaped our lives.”
Kael, now five years old, looked up at his father with wide, curious eyes. “What kind of choices, Papa?”

“The kind that require strength,” Lara answered, kneeling beside them. “And love. You’ll make those choices one day too.”

Kael nodded solemnly, his small hand reaching out to grasp Ryker's. "I'll make you proud."

Ryker's chest swelled with pride as he ruffled Kael's dark hair. "You already do."

A Celebration of Unity

To honour the strength of the pack and the bright future ahead, Ryker and Lara organized a grand celebration in the great hall. It was a feast unlike any other, with long tables laden with food, music filling the air, and laughter echoing through the mansion.

Kael ran through the crowd, his laughter infectious as he played with the other pups. Jessie, now firmly established as Ryker's beta, watched with a grin as the young heir commanded the room with ease.

"He's a natural," Jessie said, raising his glass to Ryker.

Ryker nodded; his arm wrapped around Lara's waist. "He takes after his mother."

Lara laughed, shaking her head. "And his father."

The Dance of the Alphas

As the night wore on, the music slowed, and the crowd began to drift toward the dance floor. Ryker turned to Lara; his grey eyes gleaming.
"May I have this dance?" he asked, offering her his hand.

Lara smiled, placing her hand in his. "Always."
The pack watched in awe as their alphas moved together, their connection evident in every step. The love between them was a beacon, a reminder of what they had fought for and what they would continue to protect.

As Ryker twirled Lara under the soft glow of the lanterns, he leaned down, his voice a low rumble. "You're my everything, Lara." Her hands roamed his chest, feeling the sharp dip of each muscle, as he captured her mouth in a deep, claiming kiss.

"And you're mine," she whispered in his ear, her heart full.

The Legacy Lives On

As the celebration wound down, Ryker and Lara stood together on the balcony overlooking the forest. Kael was asleep in his mother's arms, his soft glow a comforting presence.

"Do you think he's ready for what's to come?" Lara asked softly.

Ryker placed a hand on her shoulder, his grey eyes steady. "With us as his parents? He'll be more than ready."

Lara smiled, her wolf purring softly in agreement. "We've built something beautiful here, Ryker."

"We have," he replied, his voice filled with pride. "And it's only the beginning."

As the moon rose high in the sky, casting its light over the forest, Ryker and Lara stood together, their son cradled between them. The strength of their bond, their pack, and their love was unshakable, a legacy that would endure for generations to come.

Chapter 43: The Next Chapter Begins

The pack thrived in the years following the battle at the ruins. Peace had settled over their territory, and the unity they'd fought so hard to maintain was stronger than ever. Kael had become the heart of the pack—a bright, glowing symbol of hope and strength. As he grew, his unique abilities began to shine in ways no one could have anticipated, and the pack rallied behind him with fierce loyalty.

But life in the pack was never without its challenges, and for Ryker and Lara, the balance between leadership, family, and love was constantly shifting.

Updates on the Pack

The great hall was alive with activity. Wolves moved through the space, laughter and conversation filling the air as pack members shared stories and prepared for the evening's feast. Jessie stood near the hearth, his arms crossed and a rare grin on his face as he spoke with Maeve.

"Still running patrols like a drill sergeant?" Maeve teased, her eyes glinting with humour.

Jessie chuckled, shaking his head. "Someone must keep these pups in line. Besides, it keeps me sharp."

"You're sharper than ever," Maeve said, her tone softer now.

Jessie's grin faltered for a moment before he looked away, his wolf growling softly in his mind. Their connection had deepened since the battle, but neither of them had addressed it directly.

Across the hall, Lara watched them with a small smile. "Do you think they'll ever figure it out?"

Ryker stood beside her, his hand resting lightly on her waist. "Jessie's stubborn, but Maeve will break through eventually."

Lara laughed softly, leaning into him. "He deserves to be happy."

"We all do," Ryker said, pressing a kiss to her temple.

Kael.

Kael, now eight years old, was the centre of attention as he raced through the great hall with a group of pups trailing behind him. His energy was boundless, and his laughter echoed like music through the space.

"He's growing up so fast," Lara said, her voice tinged with both pride and wistfulness.

Ryker nodded, his grey eyes following his son's movements. "He's going to be an incredible leader one day."

Lara smiled, her hand resting on Ryker's arm. "With you as his father, how could he not be?"

"And with you as his mother," Ryker added, his voice filled with warmth.

Kael ran up to them, his blue eyes bright as he tugged on Lara's hand. "Mama! Papa! Come play with us!"

Lara laughed, ruffling his dark hair. "In a bit, sweetheart. Let your father and me finish our grown-up talk."

Kael pouted but nodded, racing off to join his friends again.

A Romantic Escape

Later that evening, as the pack settled into the feast, Ryker and Lara slipped away from the noise and laughter. The forest was quiet, the moonlight casting a soft glow over the trees as they walked hand in hand along a familiar path.

"It's been a while since we had a moment like this," Lara said, her voice soft.
Ryker squeezed her hand, his wolf purring in agreement. "Too long. We've been busy."

They reached a small clearing, the same one where they'd shared so many private moments over the years. Ryker turned to her, his eyes glinting in the moonlight.

"You've done so much for this pack," he said, his voice low and steady. "For me. For Kael. Sometimes I don't know how I got so lucky."

Lara smiled, stepping closer and wrapping her arms around his neck. "You're everything to me, Ryker. You and Kael."

Ryker leaned down, capturing her lips in a kiss that was slow and consuming. The world around them faded, their bond pulling them closer as the moonlight bathed them in silver.

As they walked back toward the mansion, the soft sounds of the pack's celebration reaching their ears, Lara slowed her steps.

"Ryker," she said, her voice hesitant but filled with wonder.

He turned to her, his brows furrowing slightly. "What is it?"

Lara placed a hand on her stomach, her blue eyes wide and shining. "I think… I think I'm pregnant."

Ryker's wolf growled softly, his grey eyes darkening as he stepped closer. "Are you sure?"

Lara nodded, her hand trembling slightly. "I just know."

Ryker pulled her into his arms, his voice low and filled with emotion. "Another pup," he murmured, his lips brushing against her hair.

They stood there in the moonlight, their love and excitement filling the air. But in the distance, beyond the safety of their territory, a shadow moved through the forest, unseen and silent. Lara felt something was off, but she couldn't put her finger on what.

The peace they had fought so hard for would not last forever.

www.ingramcontent.com/pod-product-compliance
Lightning Source LLC
Chambersburg PA
CBHW020947310726
48980CB00001B/85
* 9 7 8 0 4 7 3 7 4 4 2 6 7 *